IN THE WINGS

By

Ruthe Ogilvie

Order this book online at www.trafford.com
or email orders@trafford.com

Most Trafford titles are also available at major online book retailers.

Printed in the United States of America.

ISBN: 978-1-4269-3606-7 (sc)
ISBN: 978-1-4269-3607-4 (e)

*Our mission is to efficiently provide the world's finest, most comprehensive book publishing
service, enabling every author to experience success. To find out how to publish your book,
your way, and have it available worldwide, visit us online at www.trafford.com*

Trafford rev. 09/16/2010

 www.trafford.com

North America & international
toll-free: 1 888 232 4444 (USA & Canada)
phone: 250 383 6864 ♦ fax: 812 355 4082

I dedicate this book to my husband, Frank (Bud) Ogilvie, who supported me all the way; my sister, Rubye Macdonald, without whose urging I would never have written this or any book; Don Moses and Doug Warner, without whom I would never have known how to use the computer for writing this book.

CHAPTER 1

Andora Jordan sat huddled in the corner of the family room at her home in Palos Verdes, California. She gazed out at the ocean, listening to the waves as they rolled steadily into the shore, and hit the rocks with a resounding slap.

Something reliable, she thought. About the only thing left that you can really count on. The sound of it had always soothed her when she was troubled, but not this time. Her insides were churning. How could this have happened?

For just a moment she was tempted to jump off the cliff into the swirling waters below and find the peace that was so rudely snatched from her last night. And she might have, except for her daughter, Midge, who she knew would be devastated.

Her husband's voice still echoed in her thoughts - over and over. She blocked her ears, but his voice kept returning to haunt her. Tears filled her soft, emerald green eyes as she remembered what he told her last night.

"Andy," he said, "we have to talk."

She turned to him and smiled. "Yes, Paul, what is it?"

"We've been married for almost thirty years," he said.

Andy waited, hoping he was going to suggest going on the cruise she had longed to take. Their wedding anniversary was coming up next month. What a perfect way to celebrate!

"Our life has become stagnant," Paul explained. "We're in a rut. We both need a change - new faces, new places - " He broke off.

Here it comes! Andy thought. We're finally going on that cruise!

1

Paul rose and began to pace nervously. "We need a break from each other," he said. "I think we should - you know - date other people - get a new perspective. I'd like to date other women, and you could date other men. It should be fun."

Andy's heart almost stopped. She gulped, gaping at him, unable to move. Was she hearing right, or was she dreaming?

At first she thought he might be joking. Sometimes he would say something in all seriousness, then laugh, and she would know he was teasing. But this time it was real.

Why hadn't she seen it coming? He had been staying out late - coming home with liquor on his breath - stumbling into bed. But she had shrugged it off, thinking it must be some business problem that he didn't want to talk about just yet. She had trusted him, and felt that when he was ready he would come to her and discuss it.

Well, last night he did, but what he said completely shattered any trust she had in him. The hurt was indescribable, not to mention what it did to her self-esteem.

Andy's lips quivered as she answered him. "You want me to date other men? Commit adultery? Paul - we're married! Married people don't do that! What about our vows?"

As usual, his attitude toward her was condescending, as though he were speaking to someone who was addlebrained. "Andy, get with it!" he snarled. "We live in the twentieth century. Loads of people have open marriages!" He sighed in exasperation. "I hoped you'd be more open minded. This is the new morality, for Pete's sake!"

"No, Paul," she replied, her voice quivering, "this is just plain old fashioned immorality." She began to tremble. "Why are you suggesting such a thing? What have I done? Whatever it is," she begged, "I'll change. I'll make it up to you. Please - say you're joking."

"Don't be stupid. Why do you always feel you have to obey the rules? Get with it, Andy! You're no fun anymore."

Where had the Paul she knew gone? He seemed like a total stranger. Or perhaps she had never really known him.

In one short moment her whole life was in a shambles. Her marriage was in pieces, and she didn't know how to glue it back together again.

With a deep sound like a wounded animal she turned on her heel and sped toward the bedroom. She hurriedly undressed and crawled into bed, trying to escape from what she had just heard.

She lay there and stared at the ceiling. What does a woman do when after thirty years of what she had convinced herself was a good marriage her husband suddenly informs her she's no longer enough for him? He wants his freedom to pursue other women, and expects her to do the same with other men.

No divorce. No separation. Nothing like that. This would be their home as it always had been. All he wanted was his freedom to come and go as he pleased, date other women, and "have fun."

Andy had been born and brought up in New England, and the very suggestion rubbed her strict moral code the wrong way. How could Paul even suggest such a thing?

Up to this time Andy's married life had been devoted to her home and family. This had occupied and consumed her to the extent that she had put everything else on hold. What a mistake! she lamented.

Andy and Paul had been barely out of their teens when they married. She had been stunned to find herself pregnant so soon after marrying Paul. Midge, their only child, was born on Andy's twenty-first birthday, only eight and a half months after the wedding, and Andy often said she was the best present she had ever received.

As Andy lay there waiting for sleep to overtake her, she recalled Paul's reaction when she had told him she was pregnant.

Total shock! His voice had that same tone that it had tonight. "So soon?" he gasped. "That's ridiculous!"

"Paul, I saw the doctor today and he confirmed it."

Paul sounded incriminating. "Couldn't you have been more careful? I'm not ready for this."

Andy responded with amusement. "Paul," she reminded him, "I didn't do this on purpose. These things happen."

"I'm going for a walk," he said, leaving Andy feeling she had let him down.

Two hours later he returned with a small football tucked under his jacket. He walked over to Andy and kissed her on the forehead. "Make sure it's a boy."

Andy felt a great sense of relief. He's accepted the baby.

Paul was attentive during Andy's pregnancy. He often fondled the football he had bought and smiled as he tossed and caught it. "I'll teach him to play football. He'll be Captain of the team, just like me." He actually reached the point where he was looking forward to the appearance of "Paul, Jr.," as he called him.

Then the morning came when she woke him up at two A.M. and told him she was in labor.

"What? Don't be silly. The baby isn't due for two more weeks!" He turned over to go to sleep again.

"Paul, please drive me to the hospital. The pains are getting closer. There's no time to call a cab," she gasped. "This baby is getting very impatient."

"Oh, for Pete's sake!" he exclaimed. "Why did you have to get pregnant, anyway? This had better be real!"

When Andy described to the doctor what was going on, she told her to get to the hospital right away.

Paul stuck by Andy's side until they wheeled her into the delivery room. When it was all over the doctor followed Andy into her room to make sure she was comfortable. Sixteen hours of labor had taken its toll on her. But when the nurse put the baby into her arms, it made up for the whole ordeal.

Paul waited at Andy's doorway, anxious to get a glimpse of his new son.

Andy remembered hearing the doctor say to Paul, "Congratulations! The baby is finally here."

Paul was so excited. "When can I see my son - Paul Jr.?"

"I think Pauline would be more appropriate," the doctor chuckled. "You have a beautiful daughter."

Paul was angry. "It was supposed to be a boy! How can a girl play football! I have to see my wife!" He pushed past the doctor and rushed into Andy's room.

He found Andy propped up against the pillows, tired but happy. In her arms she held her newborn daughter as if she would never let go. "Paul," she said, "meet your daughter."

"What happened?" he raged. "You were supposed to have a boy! How could you do this to me?"

Andy was shocked. "Paul - it wasn't my fault. The father is the one who determines the sex of the child."

"Oh! So now you're trying to blame me!"

Andy tried to reason with him. "Don't you want to see your daughter? She's so beautiful."

Much to Andy's disappointment, Paul backed away. "No, Andy. You let me down. I don't care what she looks like, she's not a boy." With that he turned and walked out of her room and the hospital. He didn't return for a week.

At first Andy was deeply hurt. But soon her delight with her newborn filled the empty days when Paul didn't bother to visit. He'll get over it and love the baby once we get home, she figured.

When the day arrived for him to take her home he completely ignored his baby daughter. Through the years Andy had hoped this would pass, but it never did.

Midge was grown now, living away from home for many years on her own, and Andy felt very much alone.

As Andy pondered these things Paul entered the bedroom, ready to retire. When he crawled into bed, she turned away from him and cried herself to sleep.

It was still dark when Paul arose early the next morning. "Andy," he said, "I have to go to the office and take care of a few things. I'm going to New York on the noon plane. I'll be gone a month - maybe longer. I'll be in touch."

He bent over to kiss her as usual, but she turned her head away, too deeply hurt to respond.

Habit, she thought. He doesn't love me. How can he act as though nothing has changed? Nothing was the same, and she had the feeling it never would be again.

He left no forwarding address.

The house seemed empty. Andy felt completely cut off - as though someone close to her had died. What if I should need him for something - an emergency - anything?

She pushed away the mental anguish. If he didn't care enough to tell me where he's staying, why should I care? she thought bitterly. All those years meant nothing to him.

She turned over and sank down into the comforting escape of sleep. It was just beginning to get light outside when she woke up again a half hour later.

She felt heavy with grief. She wanted to scream. She had hoped when she retired last night that she would wake up to find it was all a horrible nightmare. But it wasn't.

She tried mentally to push away the dawn and go back to the darkness that would let her escape into sleep again, so she wouldn't feel the utter degradation that had swept over her last evening. She felt discarded, cast off, used.

But no matter how hard she prayed for the anesthetic called sleep, it eluded her, and she finally gave up. By this time the sun had burst through the window, and she reluctantly arose.

She felt like a robot merely going through the motions, not even remembering when she showered and dressed. She wondered why she even bothered to get up. What did she have to look forward to now?

The phone suddenly rang so loud she thought she would jump right out of her skin. It brought her sharply back to reality as she reached out and picked it up. "Hello?" she said, hoping whoever it was wouldn't notice the sadness and utter despair in her voice.

It was her daughter, Midge. She had always had an uncanny sense that knew when her mother was hurting, and this time was no exception. She never had trouble discerning her thoughts regardless of the miles between them. "Are you all right, Mom?" she asked in a concerned voice.

Andy swallowed hard, choking back the tears. "Yes, dear, I'm fine," she replied. She tried to sound cheerful, but her voice broke as she answered her daughter.

"Don't try to fool me, Mom. I'm coming over. I know something's wrong. Don't try to stop me," she said as her mother protested. "I want to know what's going on. I'll be there in an hour."

She hung up, leaving a speechless Andy holding the phone in her hand. She rose and went into the bathroom to check on her hair and makeup. Her eyes were red from crying.

I mustn't project my gloom on Midge, she thought. Andy was a very private person, extremely reluctant to dump her troubles on anyone else, especially her daughter. She opened the cabinet and found some eye drops.

As she looked in the mirror, her pretty face stared back at her. She had some wrinkles now, and her jaw line was sagging a little, but she was comfortable with the way she looked. Her mousey blond hair was combed back from her face in a very plain, schoolmarm style, but her green eyes, even without mascaraed lashes to frame them, had the wide-eyed, appearance of an innocent school girl.

Midge often chided her, and tried to coax her into having a complete make over, including a facelift, but Andy had resisted. However, even though she was close to what some people would refer to as middle-aged - she was as slim as when she had married Paul at the age of twenty.

She went quickly into the bedroom and put on the outfit she bought two days ago. Was it only two days? It seemed like another century.

She remembered how happy and lighthearted she had felt when she spied the jumpsuit on the rack. It was just what she had been looking for. When she tried it on in the store, she was pleased with the way it looked on her trim figure. She had planned to wear it the next time she and Paul went out to dinner. Now she felt she had bought it for nothing.

But she decided to put it on, anyway, hoping it would perk up her spirits and help to hide the deep hurt.

She went into the kitchen to make herself a cup of coffee and wait for Midge.

CHAPTER II

Paul settled back in his comfortable seat in First Class. The plane took off on time, and he was on his way to New York.

He smiled with contentment and patted his jacket pocket. In it was his severance check of several thousand dollars which his company had given him, and his pension, which amounted to more than thirty thousand. And he had just closed out his and Andy's joint account which totaled half a million dollars. He planned to put the money into a private bank account where no one could find it - one that would give a higher rate of interest.

He congratulated himself that he had finally found the courage to break away from Andy. He had been tempted many times in the past to leave and call the marriage quits. When they were first married he had been elated at having won Andy away from her fiance. What was that guy's name? Oh, yes - Jim Rogers.

He had been happy for a while, but the triumph he had felt soon wore thin. In the past months the boredom had become unbearable. There was no excitement left. Andy wasn't fun anymore. He needed new conquests to feed his ego.

After Midge was born everything changed. If only Midge had been a boy things would have been different, he mused. He refused to blame himself for any of this. It's Andy's fault. She let me down. She should have given me a son. I would have taken him on golf outings, but what can a girl do? He completely ignored the fact that Midge had become an accomplished golfer with a six handicap - better than Paul, whose handicap was only twenty. She's not a boy. In Paul's mind that was all that mattered.

But just as he had made up his mind to leave Andy, her parents were killed in an accident, and she had inherited their beautiful house by the sea where they were now living.

This suited his lavish life style. He couldn't give up this posh home, so he decided to stay. He figured he could still carry on with his illicit affairs, and Andy would be none the wiser.

She's so naive! he sneered. She still believes in marriage vows. Doesn't she know they're just words? As often as he could he went on golf outings and so-called business trips - any excuse to get away for his flings with whatever woman had caught his fancy for the moment.

He had made it clear to Andy last night that he wanted them to stay married. He needed this home to come back to. He wouldn't always be in New York. How he wished that he, instead of Andy, had inherited this beautiful home in Palos Verdes. He would have quit the marriage years ago.

It was seven-thirty in the evening, New York time, when the plane landed at Kennedy Airport on Long Island. Paul picked up his luggage at the carousel and went outside. A limousine was waiting to drive him and any other passengers that were going to the Waldorf Astoria. As it turned out, Paul was the only one.

It was dusk, and the lights were just coming on as the limo approached the city. Paul settled back and breathed deeply, enjoying his freedom. An array of liquor bottles stretched across a glass-enclosed shelf directly in front of the glass partition that separated him from the driver. He leaned forward and slid open the glass door. He reached for one of the bottles and an ice cube and poured himself a Scotch before settling back to enjoy his drink. This was different from the life style in California. More the life style that he liked. Sophisticated - exciting - not so laid back.

It took just under an hour from the time they left the airport until they pulled up in front of the Waldorf Astoria. A porter came out and opened the door of the limousine.

"Good evening, Mr. Jordan," he greeted Paul. "We've been expecting you." He held the door open for him to get out. "You're already checked in," he told him. "Here's the key to your suite. I'll be up with your luggage in just a moment."

Paul thanked him and entered the hotel. As he walked through the lobby he looked around. The rich decor and furnishings were more like London than New York with its Old World ambience.

Paul strolled over to the elevator. He had asked for a suite that overlooked the city. As he entered his room he could see the lights from the skyscrapers twinkling at him.

He walked over to the window. The brightly lit buildings could be seen in all their splendor. He could even see the East River off in the distance. This is the life! he cheered.

His luggage arrived and he hung up his clothes in the spacious closet. He quickly changed from his casual travel clothes to the expensive silk and cashmere suit he had bought a month ago in Los Angeles. He was expecting his date any minute.

He had just taken a final look in the mirror when he heard a knock on the door. A beautiful fashion model in her twenties stood there smiling at him. Paul grinned. How he loved to be seen with a beautiful, chic-looking young woman on his arm! "Hi, Chris. Come in and make yourself comfortable. What would you like to drink?"

"Whatever you're having will be fine," she said, and strode past him with the typical model walk she would use on a runway.

Paul went over to the private bar that was stocked with all kinds of liquor and wine. He poured them each a Scotch on the Rocks and joined her by the window.

"Where would you like to eat?" he asked.

"Some place nice," she told him.

He finished his drink and picked up the phone to dial the Concierge. "I just got in town," Paul told him. "Where would you suggest eating dinner? A really nice place. Money is no object."

"There are many fine restaurants," the Concierge told him. "I would suggest the Top Of The Sixes on Sixth Avenue, not far from here. The view is breathtaking. You can see for miles. We can arrange for the limousine to take you there if you like."

This appealed to Paul. "What time is it now?" he asked.

"It's nine o'clock, Sir. If you're ready to leave, I can arrange for you to dine at nine-thirty."

"Perfect!" Paul exclaimed. "Make the reservation for two. We'll be down in ten minutes."

CHAPTER III

An hour from the time she called, Midge rang Andy's doorbell. She lived only fifty miles and two freeways away. She stood there looking like a younger carbon copy of her mother as Andy opened the door.

Andy braced herself and put on her best smile. But no matter how hard she tried, she couldn't fool Midge, who greeted her mother warmly.

As soon as Midge was inside the house she took Andy by the hand and led her to a comfortable chair in the family room which adjoined the kitchen. "Now - - what's this all about?" she asked. She waited. "Come on, out with it!"

Andy rose and walked around the peninsula shaped countertop and over to the stove, turning her back to hide the tears that glistened in her eyes. "Would you like some coffee, dear?" she asked.

"Mom!" Midge chided her. "Stop changing the subject and tell me what's going on!"

Andy could no longer hold back the tears. She broke down, sobbing uncontrollably. This was the very thing she swore she wouldn't do, but Midge's deep concern was too much, and her wall of bravado crumbled.

Midge rose and took her mother in her arms. "Oh, Mom," she said tenderly, "what has that husband of yours done now?"

Andy brushed away the tears and sat down. "Your father's gone to New York," she told Midge. "We had a discussion last night and he wants us to live separate lives."

Midge gulped. "A divorce?"

"Oh, no, nothing like that," Andy assured her. "He just wants his

11

freedom to come and go as he pleases, date other women - an open marriage. He wants me to date other men. He thinks we're in a rut."

Midge rose from her chair, fists clenched. She walked over to the window and looked out at the ocean. She stood there for fully a minute, saying nothing.

Andy could see the struggle that was going on as Midge did her best to control her anger and disgust.

But it finally got the better of her and she turned back to her mother. "That creep!" she exploded. "Mom, that's not your style! He wants it both ways, doesn't he? A wife to do his cooking, shopping, and laundry, and his fun-fun things on the side!"

Andy was shocked. "Midge, he's your father!"

"My father!? He was never a father to me! If it hadn't been for you I would have run away long ago. He wanted a boy, remember? You'd think I didn't exist! Oh, you more than made up for it, but it's time you woke up and realized he's not the man you've fooled yourself into believing. He's selfish - undependable." She paused, then came right out with it. "Mom - he never deserved you. You're the best thing that ever happened to him, and he never had the sense to appreciate it. I'm sorry if this sounds harsh, but I think this might be the best thing that could have happened to you! I think he did you a favor! He's set you free!"

Andy burst into tears again. "How can you say that?" she sobbed. "He was my life! Now I'm alone!"

"You never had a life while you and he lived together!" Midge exclaimed. "You were always bowing to his every whim. And what about you?" She turned back to the window and looked out at the ocean once again. Her voice broke. "Mom, remember how you always wanted to go on a cruise? Did he ever take you? No! He always had a golf outing he had to go on. Or a business trip. Did he ever take you along? No!" She whirled around trembling with anger and faced Andy again. "How do you know he wasn't carrying on with his secretary? Didn't she always go with him on these business trips?"

Andy was overcome with this barrage of accusations against Paul. "Please!" she begged. "Don't accuse your father of such awful things. They're not true!"

Midge was frustrated. "Mom, wake up! He's not worth one tear! Mom, please," she begged, "listen to me. It's time you lived a little. I've got a great idea. Why don't you go on that cruise you always wanted to take? I bet you'd have a better time without him than with him. Maybe you'll even meet someone who'll appreciate you. You never know what might be waiting for you in the wings."

Andy looked around. The house seemed empty and lonely, and suddenly the thought of getting away for a while seemed strongly tempting. "Maybe you're right," she sighed. "Your father said he'd be gone for at least a month - maybe longer. And he said we should both come and go as we pleased. I have that 'mad money' that Aunt Phoebe left me. I could use some of that." Her eyes lit up with hope. "Why not?"

She reached for the phone. "I'd like the number for Transcontinental Travel, please," she told the operator. She was put on hold.

"I'm way ahead of you," Midge said with a gleam in her eye. Reaching into her handbag she pulled out a brochure. "Here," she said, handing it to her mother. "I picked this up on my way over here. I had a feeling you might be interested." She snorted. "Only I hoped that Dad might finally take you. I should have known better!"

It was a brochure on a round-the-world cruise. When Andy saw it, she gasped. "This is a three-month cruise!" she exclaimed as she handed it back to Midge. "I can't be gone that long! Your father might be home by then!" She quickly hung up the phone.

Midge's patience had run out. She exploded. "Mom, when are you going to do some of the things you want to do? Did Dad consult you when he decided to go to New York? He didn't even tell you where he could be reached. Wake up and smell the ocean breezes, Mom! Don't miss the boat!" She giggled. "No pun intended!"

This struck Andy funny, and she laughed for the first time since Paul left. "You're right," she agreed. "Give me that brochure! Round-the-world cruise, here I come!" she said, gritting her teeth. "I guess two can play this game!"

Suddenly her newly found courage left her and she looked with pleading at Midge. "Do you think you could come with me?" she asked. "I hate to go by myself. I've always had your father with me. I've never done anything without him since we were married."

"Mom, going alone is just what you need! Besides, I couldn't get away from my job for that long. But I'll go shopping with you. A whole new wardrobe will be just the thing to perk you up. And you're going to get that complete makeover if I have to drag you into the salon myself!"

She dialed the number for Transcontinental Travel that the telephone operator had given her, and handed the phone to Andy.

The agent answered on the second ring. "Yes," she said, "may I help you?"

For just a moment Andy hesitated. What am I doing? she thought. Then she plunged in. "My daughter just brought me a brochure on your cruise around the world, and I was wondering - do you have an outside cabin on your next sailing?"

The agent chuckled. "You're in luck!" she informed Andy. "I just had a cancellation."

Andy hesitated again. "When does it sail?"

"Three weeks from today at eleven AM."

"Oh," Andy exclaimed, "that's much too soon! When is the next sailing?"

"Not until month after next," the agent said. She sounded disappointed. "Are you sure you can't make it for this sailing?"

Midge picked up the extension. "This is her daughter. What's the problem?" she asked, ignoring Andy's protests.

"Your mother says she can't possibly be ready to sail in three weeks. It's too bad. I just had a cancellation. It's one of our best cabins. She could have it at a discount."

"She'll be there!" Midge said in a determined voice. "I'll see to it that she is!"

"Oh! Perfect!" The agent sounded relieved.

"Yes," Midge agreed. "You don't know how perfect it is. We'll be in this afternoon and make arrangements." She hung up and whirled around to face her mother. "This is great!" she exclaimed. "I couldn't have planned it better myself! Come on! We have work to do! You're going to have a complete makeover, including a facelift!"

Andy was appalled. "But - but - there isn't time!" she stammered. "It will take weeks to get an appointment!"

"No, it won't!" Midge promised. "I know just the one to do it. I've been dating a plastic surgeon. He's wonderful! He'll squeeze you in if I ask him, even if he has to do it at night!"

Midge had the phone in her hand before Andy could protest. A helpless Andy listened while Midge explained the situation to Dr. John Deacon. "Thanks, John," Andy heard her say. She turned to Andy with a triumphant smile on her face. "He says he'll cancel his golf date and perform the surgery day after tomorrow. You have to have blood tests this afternoon. Then you're all set!"

In a daze, Andy found herself agreeing.

They had a wonderful day shopping, having lunch at the nicest restaurant in town, and making arrangements at the travel agent's office for Andy's upcoming trip. John Deacon made sure the blood tests were rushed through.

As soon as everything was done, Midge steered Andy toward the most expensive salon in the neighborhood. Soon her long hair had been cut and shaped into the latest short fashion, and the drab hair had been highlighted to a beautiful blond. The operator showed her how to make up her eyes and face, and Andy emerged from the salon looking like a different person.

Midge stared in wide-eyed wonder. "Mom! Is that you? Where have you been hiding? Just wait until you see how you look day after tomorrow! The facelift will be just the finishing touch you need!"

Now that Andy had made up her mind to go, she was caught up in an excitement that last night she had thought was impossible when Paul had come to her with his terrible ultimatum.

As they walked toward the car, she suddenly stopped. "I haven't told your father yet! He'll be wondering where I am!"

"Mom, don't worry about it." Midge sounded a little miffed. "I think it's best if you don't contact him right now. The sound of his voice could send you into a tailspin."

Andy sighed in resignation. "I couldn't contact him, anyway. He didn't leave an address or phone number."

Midge interrupted. "Just turn on your answering machine. If he gets curious enough he'll call me. I'll be only too glad to tell him you went on a long overdue and well deserved vacation."

"You'll tell him where I am, won't you?"

"Mom," she chided, "you need this time to yourself. It will do him good to wonder for a change. He's had everything his way long enough." She looked at her watch. "I have to get back to the office. I'll pick you up day after tomorrow and drive you to John's office. After the operation is over, I'm driving you to my condo and taking care of you for the next week."

Two days later at seven o'clock sharp in the morning Andy stood at the window and watched as Midge drove into the yard. She opened the door feeling very nervous. "I'm not sure about this," she told her daughter. "I think I'm okay the way I am, especially with the new make over."

Midge reached out for her mother's hand and dragged her out to the car. "Mom," she chided, "John gave up his day of golf just to accommodate you. He'll probably never speak to me again if you back out now."

"You're making me feel guilty," Andy pouted.

"Good!" Midge exclaimed. "You're going on this cruise looking so great! It's just the boost you need for your self-esteem. Come on! We have an appointment to keep!"

Three hours later Andy emerged from the operating room hanging on to the nurse's arm, her face partially bandaged.

Dr. John Deacon came into the reception room, a pleased grin on his face. Although he was four years older than Midge, at first glance he appeared too young to be such a successful plastic surgeon. He had graduated from the University of Plastic Surgeons when he was thirty, and had been practicing for two years. His reputation had spread fast, and brought him many satisfied patients.

He looked at Midge and spoke with enthusiasm. "It came out great! A very dramatic result! Here's a list of things to do for your mother. I want to see her in a week to remove the stitches. After that it's simply a matter of time - two weeks more should do it - and she'll be ready to sail on schedule."

"Thanks, John," Midge answered. "I owe you."

John smiled at her fondly. "You don't owe me a thing. I was glad to do it. Your mother is getting a raw deal, and anything I can do to help her will be worth it."

The following week sped by quickly. Midge rented some movies which they watched together at night, and John joined them whenever he could. He and Andy hit it off like old friends.

The day for the unveiling came, and Midge drove Andy to John's office. The slight swelling had gone down, and John carefully removed the bandages. Andy hardly knew when the stitches came out.

A smile broke over John's face as he gazed at her. "Voila!" he exclaimed. "One of the best jobs I've ever done! Andy, you're a positive knockout! I might even fall in love with you myself if I hadn't met Midge first!"

Andy smiled faintly at his joke and asked for a mirror. As she took it from John she hesitated, afraid of what she might see. "John," she said, "I want Midge here when I see myself for the first time. I need her support."

"Go get Midge," John told the nurse. "I want to see her face when she first sees her mother."

In a few seconds Midge was in the room with Andy and John. "Oh, Mom!" she exclaimed in a hushed tone. "You're positively ravishing!" Her eyes filled with tears as she turned to John. "Thank you - thank you!" she said as she walked over and kissed him. She turned back to her mother. "Mom, what are you waiting for? Look at yourself!"

Andy lifted the mirror up to her face. Gone were the wrinkles and sagging, and in their place was a radiantly beautiful woman.

She frowned. "I'm not sure your father will like this," she said timidly. "I don't look the same."

"Well, I can't wait to see his face," Midge snorted. "He made the biggest mistake of his life, but it shouldn't take all this to make him sit up and take notice. That's not love!" Bitterness crept into her voice, and she turned away.

John walked over and put his arm around her. "Midge, I know how you feel. But look forward to the future, and help your mother to do the same. There's no point in looking back. That's past history." He turned to Andy. "I want you to stay out of the sun for the next two weeks. After that you'll be ready for anything."

Andy rose and faced him. "Will you be there to see me off?"

John hugged her. "You couldn't keep me away!" he promised.

The next two weeks passed by so fast Andy was hardly aware of it. Any misgivings she might have had were quickly eclipsed by the excitement over the upcoming trip. She had wanted this cruise for such a long time, and now she was actually going. She pinched herself to make sure it was true.

Each day she looked more beautiful and radiant, and she finally admitted that Midge had been right.

She was back in her own home now, and she insisted that Midge accept the dates she had planned with John. "I'm fine," she assured her daughter. "You've given up enough of your life for me. Now scoot!"

There was still no word from Paul, but she felt relieved. She was afraid he might try to talk her out of it. In the past three weeks since Paul left she had found a courage and determination that surprised her, and she wanted nothing to interfere with her newly found independence.

Let him sow his wild oats! Now it's my turn!

CHAPTER IV

Andy was packed and ready to go two days before the sailing. She felt a pang, wishing Paul were going with her, but she quickly squelched it. I need this time to myself.

As she was packing, she found a large manila envelope in her bottom drawer - an almost finished novel she had been compiling over the years, plus a complete outline for the final chapter. It needed some finishing touches and a lot of editing.

She had been tempted to throw it away, but an inner voice told her to keep it - she might want to finish it some day. On an impulse, she threw it into her suitcase. I'll work on it while I'm on the cruise. I'll probably have nothing else to do. Three months is a long time.

The morning of the sailing Midge and John arrived at Andy's house at eight o'clock. They planned to board with Andy and have breakfast together in the lavish dining room.

Each passenger was allowed one guest. Andy's guest would be Midge. But whose guest would John be? When she asked Midge, she was told it had been taken care of.

Before going to the dining room, Midge suggested that they check out Andy's cabin. Andy gasped with pleasure when she first saw it. It was a suite situated on one of the top decks, and had all the amenities of a five-star hotel.

They entered a pleasant sitting room. Champagne and a huge basket of fruit with pate and hors d'oeuvres sent by the travel agent were neatly arranged on the table. There was a small refrigerator to put whatever food was left over to snack on later when hunger attacked her.

Beyond the sitting room, the bedroom had a picture window that faced the ocean, and sliding glass doors leading out to a spacious terrace. The bath, with a spa and shower, was much larger than they expected to see on an ocean liner. On the wall of the bathroom was a phone, and another one in the bedroom beside the bed. In the sitting room a television set faced the divan, and on a table beside it was a cordless phone that could be taken out to the terrace.

"Oh, Mom!" Midge exclaimed. "This is great! Wouldn't Dad be green with envy!"

Andy couldn't hold back a reluctant grin of revenge in spite of herself.

John opened the bottle of champagne and poured some in each flute. They had just begun to toast when they were interrupted by a knock on the door.

When Andy opened it, a tall, handsome, distinguished looking man about her age stood there. He looked vaguely familiar. "Yes?" she said. "What can I do for you?"

The man smiled. "Andy, don't you know me?"

Andy blinked and took another look. Her eyes widened in surprise. "Jim? Jim Rogers?"

He hadn't changed much in the thirty years since she last saw him. His hair was slightly grey at the temples, but his eyes were the same vivid blue she remembered, and the kindly twinkle was still there.

Jim grinned and held out his arms. Before Andy knew it she was being embraced warmly. "Welcome to the cruise!" he said. "I have the cabin next door. We'll be seeing a lot of each other. I'm traveling alone, and it gets to be a real downer after a while."

Andy sent an accusing look in Midge's direction. "You planned this, you little dickens!" she said.

Midge didn't deny a thing. "Guilty as charged!" she replied. "Mom, Jim needs you just as much as you need him right now!" She was at the door before Andy could start the introductions. "Hi!" she greeted him. "I'm Midge Jordan, Andy's daughter. I talked with you on the phone, and we finally meet." She shook his hand and gestured toward John. "This is my friend, Dr. John Deacon. Please, come in and join us. We're just having some champagne and fruit before going to breakfast."

Jim shook hands with John. "I like this cruise already," he told Midge. He smiled warmly at Andy. "Your mother and I go back many years."

Andy was overwhelmed with a feeling of guilt. How do you act when you suddenly come face to face with the man you jilted one week before the wedding to marry someone else? She wanted to run and hide. Her thoughts went back to a past she had tried to forget. How deeply she had hurt Jim without meaning to! She still felt awkward about it. It all flashed back to her as she stood there staring at him, and for a moment she began to wonder why she did what she did.

Years ago they had been very much in love, and engaged to be married. And she would have married him except for Paul. She could still hear the pride in Jim's voice when he introduced them at a party two weeks before their wedding was to take place.

"Paul," he said, "meet my fiance, Andora."

Andy gazed at Paul in an almost hypnotic trance. She had admired him from a distance, but never thought she would be meeting him. This handsome adonis, Captain of the football team, shaking hands with her, was, though she didn't know it at the time, about to change her whole life.

As Andy found out later, Paul had a way of wanting what belonged to someone else, and she had been no exception. He had taken one look at her and moved in to stake his claim. Never mind that he might be hurting Jim. She was just another challenge.

He stood there looking like a movie star and smiled that charming smile that swept the girls off their feet. "Hi, Andora," he said, taking her hand in his. "What a pretty name!"

Andy blushed under his penetrating gaze. "Hi, yourself," she answered, trying not to show how unglued she felt under his scrutiny.

"Where have you been, and why haven't I met you before?" he teased. "You can tell me while we're dancing." He looked at Jim. "You don't mind, do you? I'm sure you can spare her for one dance."

Without waiting for an answer he put his arm around her waist and whirled her off to the dance floor, leaving a speechless Jim watching them.

As they danced, Paul looked down at Andy, flattering her with his eyes. He drew her close, and she could feel his breath on her neck. His rapt attention was mesmerizing as he whispered in her ear. "I'll bet you have a nickname that's just as pretty as your name."

Andy's heart beat a little faster as she answered him. "M-my n-nickname is Andy," she stuttered.

"That's almost as beautiful as you are," he cooed in her ear.

She blushed again, and felt guilty. *Why do I feel this way toward this stranger?* she wondered. *I'm marrying Jim in two weeks.*

They finished the dance, and Paul took her back to Jim. But before he handed her over he whispered, "I don't suppose you have a phone number?"

On an impulse she did something that surprised her. She mouthed it to him, and he quickly jotted it down in a small black book that he carried. He had called her night and day after that, and finally talked her into believing that she was in love with him instead of Jim.

Andy was very young and impressionable, and deeply flattered by his sudden infatuation and attention. In a hypnotic daze she had succumbed to his agressive persuasions. A week before she was to marry Jim, she had eloped with Paul, who was triumphant at having won her over from Jim.

So, after the whirlwind courtship and return from their sudden elopement, Andy was faced with the task of telling Jim. She arranged to meet him at a small, out-of-the-way cafe on the outskirts of town.

She shuddered as she recalled vividly the look of - first, disbelief - then disappointment and shock. "Jim, I have something to tell you. I hope you won't be too upset. Please try to understand. I - I - "

Jim looked at her, puzzled. "What is it, Andy? You look so serious."

She knew this had to be said, and the quicker she told him the sooner it would be over. She looked at him tenderly. "Jim, Paul and I were married last night."

Jim was silent for a moment before he spoke. Then he laughed. "You're kidding." He paused and waited. "You are, aren't you?"

But Andy's face told him she wasn't. She reached out and tried to take his hand in a show of sympathy, but he quickly rose from his seat. He wished her well and left. The last she heard he had left town with no forwarding address. He cut all ties. Rumor had it that he had been offered a position in Paris and had accepted it, putting as much distance as he could between himself and the cause of his deep hurt.

Andy never heard from him again until coming face to face with him now. One day she and Midge were talking girl talk, and Andy confessed the whole thing to her. But she had no idea that Midge would go this far to see that he was on this same cruise. How had she known where to contact him after all these years, when even Andy didn't know?

"Mom." Midge's voice sounded like an echo from far off as Andy snapped back to the present. "Why don't you pour Jim some champagne? Jim, help yourself to anything that's here." She turned to Andy. "I feel much better knowing you won't be alone, Mom. Jim is right next door. Isn't that great?"

Jim turned to Andy. "Do you have your seating arrangement for dinner yet?"

This was all happening too fast, and Andy was confused. "N- no. I just boarded and came right to my cabin."

"We'll take care of it when we go to breakfast," Jim told her.

There was an awkward silence. "I - I heard that you took a position with a company in France," Andy said. " Are you still living there?"

"No," he replied. "After twenty-five years I figured I'd take an early retirement. I was homesick for the States. I came back three years ago and bought a home in Santa Barbara."

"Your wife didn't come with you?" Andy asked.

"No, we're in the process of getting a divorce," he told Andy. "My wife wanted to 'find herself,' I believe is the expression she used. She stayed in France. Her old boy friend had just been widowed. I'm sure that had something to do with it."

Can he be going through the same thing I am? Andy wondered. She sensed that he was reluctant to discuss it any further, and she changed the subject. "It's nine-fifteen," she announced. "We'd better get down to breakfast if we want time to explore the ship afterwards."

Jim put his arm through Andy's. "Let's go!" Before she could protest, he marched her out the door and down the corridor toward the elevator.

The buffet was spread out on a table clear across one end of the huge dining room. Danish pastries, omelets, pancakes, waffles, eggs any way you like them, bacon, ham, coffee - there was no end to the enormous variety of food.

The maitre d' was there to take care of the dinner seatings, and Jim walked over to him, pulling Andy by the hand. "I want you to take care of this lady," he told him. "I'm sitting at table number twenty-six at the early seating, and I want her next to me. Is that okay with you?" he asked, turning to Andy. "I'll be really disappointed if it isn't."

The comical look of mock pleading on his face struck her funny, and she laughed in spite of herself. "You're impossible!" she said. "How could I refuse when you look at me like that?"

"Good!" Jim grinned. "Then it's all set. Let's go back with the others and eat."

With all the fruit and fancy hors d'oeuvres they had just had in Andy's cabin, they didn't really need any breakfast, but the sea air was already whetting their appetites. The spread was tempting, and they decided to take advantage of it and get into the spirit of the cruise.

What delicious food! It was everything the brochure had said it would be!

After breakfast they explored the whole ship. It didn't take quite an hour and a half. It was a smaller ship than some, and more intimate. They stopped in at one of the cocktail lounges to listen to the music.

Soon it was time for Midge and John to leave. The Purser had already made the first announcement for all visitors to debark.

Andy looked at her daughter. "I wish you were going with me," she pleaded.

"Mom," Midge chided, "you've been handed a great gift - time to think. Take it and use it."

She and John shook hands with Jim, hugged her mother, and were gone.

Andy was left alone with Jim. She felt self-conscious, like a school girl on her first date.

But he smiled at her, and she relaxed. She decided then and there to enjoy this trip in spite of the heartache that had brought her here.

They went up on deck to watch the ship lift anchor and sail away on their round-the-world cruise.

CHAPTER V

It was almost noontime when the pier finally disappeared as the ship headed out to the open sea. The weather couldn't have been nicer. An exhilarating breeze suddenly picked up and caressed their faces.

Andy stole a glance at Jim. It was so comforting to have him here. She hadn't realized until this minute how much she had missed him. Or maybe she had deliberately blocked it out.

Jim smiled and turned away from the railing. "I don't know about you," he said, "but I'm famished. Must be this ocean air. What do you say we head down to the dining room and get something scrumptious to eat? How about it? Let's pig out!"

He pulled her away from the railing and toward the elevator. Other passengers were already in the dining room. The food spread was positively sinful. Even more elaborate than breakfast.

There was everything anyone could want! Not only that, but the way it was presented defied the imagination! Exotic lights played on each dish, with a fountain in the center of the huge, long table. And over to the side was a large freezer filled with all different flavors of ice cream and toppings, inviting the guests to make their own lavish sundaes!

As Andy and Jim entered the room they could hear the tumbling water from the fountain as it blended in with the music from the piano and the low murmur of happy voices. They put as much food on their plates as they felt they could handle, and went to the outside deck where tables and chairs were set up. As they ate, they watched the ocean pass by. Dolphins followed the ship, leaping out of the water and singing their sweet songs.

Andy breathed deeply. Paul and her problems seemed far away. Too bad he had to miss all this, she sighed. But I'm here, and I'm going to enjoy every minute. She shut him out of her thoughts, and turned her attention to Jim.

As soon as they finished eating, he made a suggestion. "Did you look at the bulletin board this morning? They're holding a contest on the Polynesian Deck. Anyone who wants to can hit golf balls into the ocean. You have four tries, and whoever gets the best shots wins a prize. Do you play golf?"

Andy turned her head away. She remembered how Paul had put her down the one time she tried to play golf with him. He had treated her as though she were stupid. He loved to belittle her. Consequently, she hadn't played her best. She had excused herself and gone into the club house for a good stiff drink - the first time she ever did that. She never played with him again.

Jim studied her intently. "What's the matter, Andy? If you don't play we don't have to enter the contest. It's no big deal. I just thought it might be fun."

Andy quickly pulled herself together. "Yes!" she replied. "I've never won any prizes, but let's go for it!"

"Atta girl!" Jim exclaimed. He pulled her up from the table and they headed hand in hand for the Polynesian Deck.

The event was already in progress, and suddenly Andy felt shy. "You go first, Jim," she suggested, trying to retrieve the courage she had felt only moments ago.

Jim stepped up to the rubber tee that had been placed on the mat on the floor of the deck. The railing was open, and one of the crew strapped him into a harness so he wouldn't fall overboard. He hit four beautiful drives.

Andy was up next. She hesitated for just a moment. Then, with great determination, she stepped up to the tee. The crewman strapped her in and she looked at Jim.

He smiled and nodded. Andy gritted her teeth. You get a great shot or I'll kill you! she muttered. She tried to remember what she had learned from the lessons she had taken. She took the club in her hands, gripped it as she had been taught, and went into her backswing. Remember what the teacher said - it's just like a backhand stroke in tennis, only with the left hand. Keep your head down and watch the clubhead hit the ball.

As she was about to complete the swing and follow through, she closed her eyes and prayed. She heard a resounding whack as the clubhead made contact with the ball. She had hit a beautiful drive straight out into the ocean. She wasn't prepared for the cheers from the others waiting for their turn. She grinned and made a mock bow. What a difference it makes when someone believes in you! she exulted. One down and three to go. The first one gave her the confidence she needed, and she hit three more great shots.

By the time the other contestants finished, both she and Jim had won a prize. How grateful she was for Jim's encouragement. She was beginning to see a big difference between Paul and Jim.

She felt guilty and tried to deny it.

They headed in the direction of the theater laughing and talking like a couple of teenagers. Gone were the years in between. That was then - this was now. Andy hadn't felt so lighthearted in years. How grateful she was that Jim had forgiven her.

She felt guilty again. She was having fun without Paul. How could that be?

The movie was tender and touching. Andy laughed and cried, and Jim lent her his hankie. She could see that it touched him deeply, too.

Paul would have told her she was being stupid, and walked away.

Another big difference.

When the movie was over they had just time enough to go to their cabins and dress for dinner. It was formal the first night out. The Captain was expecting the early diners for the first cocktail party just before dinner.

Andy wore a sparkling, sequined cocktail dress in a beautiful lilac color that complemented her blond hair. On her feet were silver sandals. Each one was adorned with a lilac bow. On top of her new short hair she pinned a pert, lilac bow that matched the bows on her sandals. Over her shoulders was draped the lovely mink stole that Paul had given her last Christmas.

Tears came to her eyes as she remembered. She had wanted one for a long time. Paul had just returned from one of his long business trips two days before the holidays, and brought this with him.

But Andy also remembered something she had heard Midge mutter under her breath when she opened the package.

"Something to assuage his conscience?" Midge had mumbled almost inaudibly. "Which girl friend was he with this time?"

Andy quickly shook off the memory. She threw back her shoulders and emerged from her cabin just as Jim appeared.

Jim's eyes lit up when he saw her. He was wearing a white tuxedo with a white bow tie, and looked every bit as handsome as Andy remembered when she had attended the high school prom with him many years ago. It was almost as though the past thirty years had been erased. This was a new beginning.

Arm in arm they went to the Captain's party.

The Captain stood at the door of the Lounge, and soon they were being presented to him.

Andy felt a little awkward when the Purser introduced them as Mr. and Mrs. James Rogers.

Jim, however, laughed and quickly corrected him. "We're just old friends who bumped into each other here on the cruise," he explained. "We're sitting at the same table for dinner, and decided to come to the party together."

As they stood talking to the Captain, the photographer took their picture, and told them it would be ready for them to see tomorrow morning on the display just outside the Reception Lounge.

The Lotus Lounge where the cocktail party was being held was decorated with balloons and flowers. On a hugh table at the far end, champagne was bubbling its way down from glass to glass in pyramid fashion, ready to be served to the guests. As the glasses were taken to the tables, more glasses were set up, more champagne was poured from the top, and the fountaining began all over again. The waiter led them to a table beside a window that looked out on the ocean. Hugh waves were thundering by as the ship plowed its way through, stopping for nothing. Life goes on, Andy thought, just like the waves.

The waitress approached them with two glasses of champagne.

Jim held up his glass for a toast and smiled. "Here's to a new beginning and a new friendship," he said.

Andy studied him. Why can't I erase the hurt that Paul caused as easily as Jim has forgiven me? she chided herself.

She felt a strength of character coming from Jim that she had never felt from Paul. Hush! she warned herself. Paul is your husband. She felt disloyal.

By the time they finished their champagne it was time to go to dinner. They quickly found their assigned table. It was a table for six, and soon the others joined them. After the waiter had taken their orders they introduced themselves, and were soon chatting like old friends.

Andy remembered all the evenings she had spent alone when Paul was away, and it seemed wonderful to be surrounded by gaiety and laughter. A pianist was playing Beethoven's "Moonlight Sonata" in soft tones, and a low murmur of conversation filled the room.

It was eight o'clock when Andy and Jim finished eating. They planned next to see the stage show and follow it with a movie they had both been wanting to see.

They were well on their way to the high seas by now. The ship was sailing so smoothly they hardly knew it was moving. The late diners were lined up at the door, anxious to be seated, so Andy and Jim left the dining room.

Together they strolled down the corridor to the lounge where the show was to be performed. They quickly found seats on one of the comfortable sofas directly in front of the stage. Top notch entertainers had been flown in to perform a medley of musical numbers from the latest Broadway shows.

Andy almost forgot about her problems as she watched. It was so much more than she had ever imagined she would see on board ship. She even recognized some of the stars whose pictures she had seen only in magazines.

She turned to see Jim smiling at her, and a warm, happy feeling crept over her. She quickly shook it off, thinking she was perhaps being unfaithful to Paul.

The show was over all too soon, and Andy was again feeling the deep humiliation she felt when Paul first told her what was on his mind. She struggled to hold back the tears.

As they exited the lounge, she turned to Jim. "I think I'll take a walk around the deck before going down to the movie. I need to clear my head. I'll see you at the theater."

She had been doing well so far, and Jim had promised Midge he wouldn't give Andy a chance to sink down into depression and self pity again. "Great idea!" he enthused. "I'll go with you. I could do with a little fresh air myself."

He took her arm and guided her to the door that led to the deck. He opened it for her and followed her outside.

After one complete turn around the deck they stopped by the railing. The moon was out bright, and the valleys on it were so clear it seemed that they could almost span the distance and walk through them. As the ship plowed ahead, the moonlight sparkled and glistened on the wake that it left behind, as if to say, "Not a care in the world, all is happy and bright - nothing is wrong in the world tonight."

How I wish I could feel that way, Andy thought with longing. Her thoughts kept swinging like a pendulum between hope and despair. Paul had killed their marriage, and she wondered how she could ever trust him or any other man again.

Jim breathed deeply. "Beautiful, isn't it?"

Andy swallowed a sob. "A couple of rejects!" she mumbled.

Jim looked at her thoughtfully. "What did you say?"

She shrugged her shoulders. "A couple of rejects!" she repeated with bitterness in her voice. "Isn't that what we are?"

Jim smiled. "You can be a reject if you want to. But I refuse to be. There's a lot of living to be done, and I intend to search it out and see what I come up with. I'm not going to stop living just because my wife left me. She wasn't what I thought she was. I know what you're feeling," he assured her. "I've been there. Twice," he mumbled, looking away.

Andy looked at him with a deep sense of remorse. "Oh, Jim, I'm sorry. I hurt you badly, I know. How can you ever forgive me?"

Jim stared at the ocean. "That was a long time ago," he assured her. "Time is a great healer."

"But now your wife has deserted you as well," she said, turning away. All the guilt she felt years ago when she was forced to tell him she eloped with Paul washed over her like a flood.

Jim turned back to her. "But we're here together now," he reminded her, "facing the same thing. We can help each other through a rough time. Besides," he grinned, "you never know what's in the wings just waiting for you. Maybe it will be a lot better than what you and I had in our marriages. What we thought we had was a sham."

She nodded. "Paul certainly wasn't the man I thought he was, that's for sure," she agreed. "I guess I was loving someone who never really existed."

"Well, aren't you glad you found out and you've been lifted out of it? It could be the best thing that ever happened to you! To both of us."

Andy looked at him with wonder in her eyes. "That's what Midge said," she marveled.

"We can't live with a fantasy forever!" Jim told her. "I had to come to terms with the same thing. I was living with a dream - someone who wasn't what I hoped she'd be. Perhaps I was trying to make her into you," he mumbled. He shrugged it off and gazed at her. "You're a very beautiful woman. Surely you know that."

Andy was surprised. "Me? Beautiful?"

"Don't sell yourself short," Jim admonished her. He laughed. "I might even fall in love with you all over again," he joked.

"Please don't patronize me," Andy begged. "That's the last thing I need right now."

He patted her shoulder. "And that's the last thing I would do," he assured her. "I have too much respect for you." He reached for her hand. "How about going inside? That music needs to be danced to. We have half an hour before the movie begins." He pulled her toward the door.

She didn't resist. It seemed nice to have a man to lean on again, and a very nice man, at that - even though he was just a friend from the past. But wasn't that what she needed right now? She wasn't ready for anything else. Besides, she reminded herself, I'm still married. I have to be there for Paul when he comes back. She didn't want to admit that sometimes she almost wished he wouldn't. What if he leaves me again? she thought. I couldn't go through this a second time.

Suddenly she didn't feel like going into a crowded ballroom with a lot of other people. "Jim," she said, "why don't we dance out here?"

"Great idea!" He held out his arms and she melted into them. As they danced they moved as one person. He held her tightly, protectively, as though by his very presence he could shield her from the hurt she was feeling.

Andy was fully aware of what Jim was trying to do. She knew deep down that she had hurt him much more deeply than his wife had. He was coping with that more easily than the hurt she had seen on his face years ago when she broke the news to him of her elopement with Paul. Yet here he was comforting her because of what Paul had done to her. She was awed that his only concern now was for her comfort and solace.

She felt unworthy. At the same time, she couldn't help tingling with a cozy, warm feeling of contentment just being in his arms. All this, combined with her resentment and deep hurt from the damage that Paul had done to her self-esteem, suddenly washed over her like the giant waves relentlessly pounding against the side of the ship. She was drowning in a sea of confusion, being pulled down by an undertow of guilt so strong she could no longer fight it.

She dissolved into tears and broke away. "I'm sorry," she sobbed. "Please excuse me. I'm going to my cabin."

She turned and fled through the door and up the stairs to her suite, leaving Jim standing there alone.

CHAPTER VI

It was morning, and Andy sat alone on the terrace of her cabin watching the sunrise. Soon the dazzling colors of bright orange, yellow, and pink covered the sky with all their splendor as the first sliver of orange ball emerged from the sea.

Andy hadn't slept much last night. She was riddled with guilt. She found it difficult to admit that she had enjoyed herself in the company of a man other than Paul.

Jim seemed so attentive. I'm afraid he still cares, she thought. I don't want to hurt him again.

You're imagining things, she told herself. You're worrying over nothing. Jim would never be interested in you again. Not that way. Not after the way you treated him before.

She was still wearing her nightie and robe, and wasn't sure she wanted to get dressed and face the world. She just wanted to take refuge in her cabin and hide from everyone.

She reached for the manuscript of her novel which was on the table beside her. She thumbed through the pages, then put it down, unable to concentrate.

Her thoughts were interrupted by a sharp knock on her door. She jumped up and went back into the sitting room. "Who is it?" she called out.

"Andy? It's Jim. Are you almost ready to go down for breakfast? They're only serving for another hour. I've been waiting for you."

Andy sighed. "You go ahead. Thank you for waiting, but I don't think I'll bother this morning. I'm not hungry."

Jim put his mouth to the keyhole. "I can't let you do this," he chanted in sing-song fashion. "Hiding with your hurt is the worst thing you can do. I hate to eat alone. If you hurry, we can still make it."

Silence.

"They're serving pigs-in-a-blanket this morning," he teased.

My favorite breakfast - fluffy pancakes wrapped around sausages! He remembered all these years! she marveled. She started to reach for her slippers, then stopped.

"Oink-oink," he called through the door.

Andy laughed in spite of herself. "Okay," she relented. "Give me fifteen minutes. I have to shower and dress."

"Knock on my door when you're ready," he said. "Dress casual. This is vacation time."

Andy went into the bathroom and turned on the shower. The warm water felt soothing as it washed over her. She toweled off and reached for the hair dryer.

She was ready sooner than the fifteen minutes she had asked for, strangely anxious to be with Jim. He's a lot more fun than Paul, she observed. The sense of guilt attacked her again. Be careful. You're a married woman, she reminded herself, not like Jim who's getting a divorce.

I know how he must feel, she thought. This is the second time he's been dumped, and I'm to blame for the first. She refused to blame Paul for any part of it. It was all my fault, not his, she thought stubbornly. Her loss of self-esteem, which Paul had instilled in her, refused to let her blame anyone but herself.

I have no right to be happy, she lamented. What I feel for Jim is sympathy - that's all it is.

She took a last look at herself in the mirror. Her wedgewood blue split skirt and coordinating blue and white top graced her slim figure. On her feet she wore comfortable, white sport shoes with easy, convenient velcro straps. She looked like a model.

With a toss of her head she grabbed her purse and left her cabin. Maybe I don't deserve to be happy, she thought, but he does. He needs cheering up, and this is something I can do for him. Stop feeling sorry for yourself and try to cheer him up, she chided herself. He waited to take you to breakfast. You owe him that much.

She raised her hand to knock on Jim's door. Suddenly a smile tugged at the corners of her mouth. She stooped down and pursed her lips. "Oink-oink," she called through the key hole.

The door opened and there stood Jim, his face all screwed up as he used to do years ago. She always said he had a rubber face. His cheeks were filled with air, and his mouth was set like a pig's snout.

Andy collapsed against the wall in hysterics. This was just what she needed. He quickly unscrewed his face and joined her, laughing as hard as she was.

He grabbed her hand, and they pranced down the corridor chanting, "Oink-oink," as they passed other passengers. They managed to keep it up until they entered the elevator.

"They must think we're nuts!" Andy said as the elevator door slid shut.

"Oh, I certainly hope so!" Jim chimed in.

They burst out laughing again, and exited the elevator. Before going to the dining room, they stopped by the reception lounge where the pictures were on display.

As they stood there looking at their picture they heard someone remark what a handsome couple they made. Jim laughed, but Andy was embarrassed, and they made a hasty retreat to the dining room.

It was a beautiful day at sea. The air was dry, and the sun shone brightly as the ship plowed through the waves. They decided to eat outside on the deck. A marimba band was playing calypso music.

As soon as they found a table and put their plates down, Jim grabbed Andy around the waist and danced her around the deck. She was feeling in better spirits, and it showed.

When she could get her breath, she looked at him and laughed. "Thanks," she said.

"For what?" he asked.

"I know what you're doing, and it's working. You make me feel a lot better. I'm glad you're here."

His arm tightened around her. He finished swinging her around and they returned to their table, breathless and ready to eat their pigs-in-a-blanket before they got too cold.

Andy looked around, taking in everything in sight. She sighed a deep, satisfied sigh.

"A penny for your thoughts," Jim said. "Oh, I mean a dollar! I almost forgot about inflation!"

"You're impossible!" Andy laughed.

She gazed off in the distance. Paul was the furthest thing from her mind at this moment.

She looked at Jim and smiled. "I was thinking - I should write about all this sometime." She gestured toward the ocean.

Jim's eyes lit up. "Do you still write? You got the highest marks in the writing class. The teacher had great hopes for you as a future author."

Andy frowned, but quickly brushed it aside. "I've wanted for a long time to finish a novel I started twenty-eight years ago."

His eyes widened. "Why haven't you? You have the talent."

Andy hesitated. She remembered the few times she had retired to her room when some ideas came to her. Paul had always found a way to interrupt her. He needed a lost sock or shoe, or he had brought home a guest without warning her ahead of time. And she had put her unfinished novel aside while she tried to get ideas for some special dish to please the unexpected guest.

When she finally managed to steal away by herself to try and write another chapter, Paul would laugh at her attempts. "Surely you don't think you're good enough to become a novelist," he would sneer. "You'd better stick to homemaking. Being a writer takes a special kind of person, and you're not one of them."

Remembering this made Andy wince.

Jim didn't miss a beat. "What is it, Andy? Did Paul discourage you?"

Andy nodded. "He said I'd never make it, so I'd better not waste my time."

Jim turned away and gazed at the ocean, an angry look on his face. He looked as though he wanted to say something, but thought better of it.

Instead, he turned back to her and spoke in a positive tone. "You wouldn't be wasting your time, Andy. In fact, I think it's a great idea. I hope you brought a sample with you."

"I brought along what I have. I thought I might find time to finish it on the cruise."

"I'd love to read it," he told her. "I'll be glad to give you an honest critique."

Andy was doubtful. "I'm not sure it's any good. Maybe some other time."

"There's no time like the present. What's wrong with right now?"

Andy hesitated.

"Hey," he reminded her, "I'm not Paul - I'm Jim." He tilted his head to one side and grinned. "Come on," he teased, "lay it on me."

Andy gave him a long, hard look, and finally relented. "Okay," she said. "But don't say I didn't warn you. I'll bring it along tomorrow."

The rest of the day was spent doing some of the many things that the ship's crew had planned to keep the passengers busy. The first thing they did was to attend the movie they had missed last night when Andy left Jim so abruptly. After lunch they played bingo. Andy had never been lucky at winning anything at the functions she attended with Paul. But with Jim by her side she was the happy, surprised winner of seven hundred and fifty-two dollars, which she insisted on sharing with him. That night after dinner they watched another live show in the Lotus Lounge, and still another movie.

The next morning Andy was up bright and early. She felt a strange mixture of excitement and self-doubt, not knowing which emotion was strongest. Paul had said she was wasting her time writing, but Jim said just the opposite. Who was she to believe? When she and Jim went to breakfast she was carrying a note pad and a large manila envelope with the novel and the notes she had compiled over the past twenty years.

"What have you got there?" Jim asked.

"You said you wanted me to run my novel past you," Andy answered, "so here it is. After we eat we can go out on deck and you can look at it."

She had the feeling she was entering a new chapter in her life, and Jim was responsible for it. She felt an enthusiasm well up in her that had been missing for some time.

As soon as they finished breakfast they went outside. They quickly found some deck chairs and settled down. It was a bit chilly this morning, so Jim found a couple of blankets, and soon they were snuggled under them.

Andy gazed out at the ocean with a contented smile on her face. How grateful she was for Jim's interest. What a welcome change from what she had come to expect from Paul!

"Well, come on," Jim coaxed, "where is this novel you were going to honor me with?"

Andy handed the manila envelope to him. "It's hard to believe I've been working on this for twenty-eight years. I brought along a note pad to record your critique so I can study it later."

Jim opened the envelope and pulled out the pages, careful to keep the wind from blowing them away. He was quiet for about half an hour while he thumbed through them. When he finished, he stared off into space.

Andy watched him closely. It was hard to tell what he was thinking.

He put everything back into the envelope and looked at her. "What a wonderful story!" he exclaimed. "Andy, you've been wasting your time and your talent. You have a whole novel in this envelope! All you have to do is buckle down and finish it. What are you waiting for?"

"You really think it's good?" she asked timidly.

"I don't know why you've waited so long to finish it," he declared. "Or maybe I can guess," he said grimly.

"Well -" She hesitated. "It's kind of hard trying to type at home and not make typos - all the interruptions - having to retype pages. Publishers won't accept anything with mistakes -"

"A typewriter! Andy, you need a computer. It's much faster when you can see what you've written on the screen right in front of you. The editing goes much faster, too. And if you make a typo you don't have to retype the page. Just correct it on the screen and print it out. I could go on and on with the benefits of a computer. It's far superior to what a mere typewriter can do."

"I don't know how to run a computer! I don't know the first thing about computers!" she declared.

"You've got to get one, Andy. Once you get used to a computer you'll never go back to a typewriter."

"But - but - who would show me how to use it? I'm not good with machinery. It must be very difficult - - "

"Nonsense!" Jim interrupted. "I could show you in an hour." He jumped up. "I have an idea! Maybe they have one on the ship. You could get started right now!" He reached out for her hand and pulled her up from the deck chair.

Andy pulled back. "Where are you taking me?"

"We're going to find a computer, and I'm going to show you how to use it!"

"But - but -" she protested - "I can't expect them to let me use it whenever I get an inspiration!"

"You never know until you ask!" Jim said.

By this time she was on her feet, eager to find out what Jim was talking about. As they exited the deck, Jim spied a phone on the wall that had been put there for the passengers' use. He picked it up and dialed the Purser. "Do you have any computers on board that the passengers can use?" he asked.

"Yes, we have a special room," the Purser told him. "It's on the

Promenade Deck. We occasionally have writers on board who need to use them."

"I have a friend who's writing a novel," Jim explained. "Do you have any floppy disks so the story can be transferred to the computer at home?"

"Yes, Sir," the Purser assured him. "You'll find a supply in the cabinet above the computers. The text can be installed into the writer's own machine at home with no problem."

"Wonderful!" Jim exclaimed. "Just what we need! Thanks!" He hung up and turned to Andy. "Come on!" he said, taking her by the hand. "We're going to the computer room and you're going to finish writing your novel!"

They soon reached the Promenade Deck. As they entered the room they saw half a dozen computers not being used. Jim chose one that was tucked away in a corner, where Andy would have plenty of privacy.

She was amazed how quickly she learned with Jim showing her. She was a fast typist, having taken a course in an evening class when Paul was out of town. In just four hours of steady typing the first dozen chapters of the novel had been installed and filed into the word processing system in the machine.

"You're going to come here directly after breakfast each day and finish this," Jim ordered.

"But what will you do while I'm writing?"

"Just what I did this morning," he said. "I'll sit and watch you write. When you become a famous author, I can say I was with you when you wrote it. And I'll be here in case you run into a snag."

Andy looked at him with wonder. How different he is from Paul, she marveled. Why couldn't Paul be more like Jim? This time she felt less guilty. "I won't be writing all the time," she assured him.

"Of course not!" he agreed. "We've got to spend some time exploring the different ports. That will give you a lot more to write about." He grabbed her hand. "Let's get some lunch."

CHAPTER VII

From then on Andy was up at six o'clock each morning to have breakfast with Jim and go immediately to the computer room and write for a few hours. She still made time to have dinner with him, as well as seeing some of the nighttime shows and movies. She even managed to squeeze in a few days of touring at various ports just to give herself a breather from her writing, and return to it with a fresh viewpoint.

The first port they visited was in Hawaii. The ship stopped at four of the Islands - Oahu, Maui, Kauai, and last of all the big Island of Hawaii.

On the Island of Kauai they decided to take a ride in a helicopter. It was a bit frightening at first, but the pilot was so adept at flying through the narrow crevices between the mountains that soon the fear was replaced by the thrill of the magnificent scenery that surrounded them. Viewing it high above the terrain provided a much larger and awesome panorama of sea, sky, mountains, and small villages tucked inside the valleys and hills.

Andy was beginning to understand how much more she was getting out of this three month cruise than she would have on the mere two week cruise that she had hoped to take with Paul. Not only was she seeing much more, but what a wealth of ideas was unfolding before her eyes that could be included in her novel! And maybe other novels that she might write in the future! And as an added bonus she was enjoying this with Jim - someone who encouraged her, rather than putting her down and making her feel useless. Her eyes were being opened, although she wasn't ready yet to fully admit it.

After the helicopter ride they decided to stop for lunch at a seaside restaurant on the beach, rather than going back for their meal on the ship. They both ordered the fish of the day - mahi-mahi, a white fish well known in the Hawaiian Islands for its mild taste. Not a bit fishy. It was served with an aspic salad, tartar sauce, and cole slaw. Dessert was a delicious baked apple with cinnamon, laced with bourbon and topped with French vanilla ice cream.

It was a beautiful, clear day. The waves were pounding on the shore, rolling in a sea of white. Overhead were seagulls soaring and banking before diving down to catch a fish that caught their fancy.

Andy looked at Jim with a deep feeling of contentment. Almost forgotten - but not quite - was Paul's cruel rejection of her that had brought her here.

All too soon it was time to return to the ship. The crew was just about to pull up the gangplank when they boarded - just five minutes before it was time to sail.

The next port coming up was Australia. Andy had been anticipating this one ever since she first saw the brochure showing the picturesque harbor in Sydney with its incredibly blue water glistening in the bright sunlight.

They rose early in the morning and stood on the deck as they pulled in to the pier. The famous Opera House with its unique architectural design - the most recognizable landmark in all of Australia - presided majestically over the harbor.

Andy grabbed Jim's hand in an effort to contain her excitement. She and Jim both loved opera, and included in their tour were tickets to attend a presentation of "La Boheme," by Puccini, to be given that night. The three days that the ship was scheduled to stay there would allow them to see a good part of the area surrounding Sydney. They had already signed up for the special bus tours that would visit the outlying towns and suburbs. They were especially looking forward to the trip out of Melbourne to Philip Island where the fairy penguins resided.

The performance at the Opera House had been completely bought out by the tour agents before leaving the States, so the two seatings for dinner were combined to allow all the passengers to attend the opera that night.

At six o'clock Jim knocked on Andy's cabin door. He was dressed in a black tuxedo with a white shirt, a black bow tie, and black shoes.

Andy opened the door, ready to leave for dinner. Her short hair framed her lovely face. Her eyes seemed greener than usual, reflecting the emerald green gown she wore. They sparkled as brilliantly as the rhinestones scattered across the bodice of her full-length dress. Her mink stole was thrown casually over her shoulder, and in her hand she carried a beaded evening purse.

She felt a newfound joy, but at the same time guilt. Too bad Paul had to miss all this, she mused. One minute she felt light-hearted, and the next minute she was plunged into anxiety. It was hard for her to shake the feeling that she didn't deserve this. She had an awful premonition that it would be snatched away without a moment's notice. Why do I feel this way? she wondered. Was this a peek into the future? Or was it just a latent fear that made no sense at all?

She shook it off. Seeing a performance at the Opera House in Sydney was a dream come true, and she made up her mind that she would enjoy it to the fullest.

The next morning the ship docked at Melbourne. Andy and Jim were up early for breakfast. On the dock a bus waited to take them to Philip Island. It was hot, and she and Jim were dressed in light weight slacks and tee shirts as they boarded the bus.

There was much to see of the countryside as they rode through the streets and picturesque lanes on their way to the Island. They made one stop at a sheep ranch to see the ranch hands shear the sheep. Lunch was served at the farm, and they were on their way again. They arrived at Philip Island around four o'clock in the afternoon. It was beginning to get chilly, and they donned their sweaters while they waited for the penguins to emerge from the sea. The tour guide explained to them that the male penguins left early in the morning, plunging into the sea for food to bring back to their mates, who waited patiently on the shore in their small hovels. Unlike some other species, they mated for life.

Andy and Jim got the biggest kick out of seeing how each male knew just which one was his spouse. He would walk up to one of the females, look at her, shake his head, then waddle away until he found the one that belonged to him.

The first thing Andy and Jim did was to put away their cameras. The tour guide warned them not to take flash pictures. The flash would blind these delightful little creatures, and they would have to be destroyed.

They arrived back at the ship in time for dinner and a show, and then to bed.

The next day Andy was busy at the computer again.

Jim was so patient and encouraging. She could see that he was having as much fun with this as she was.

The days that stretched ahead were something they both looked forward to. Other ports they visited were New Zealand with its beautiful landscapes; Tahiti, a tropical Island in the South Pacific, famous for its monsoons and quaint villages; Fiji, where they managed to get in nine holes of golf; and Japan, where they fed the tame deer in Nara. Every port had something new to see, and Andy jotted down notes every night.

One port of particular interest was Dalian, China. As the ship pulled into port she and Jim stood at the railing waiting to get off the ship. On the pier were at least twenty young Chinese girls, no more than twelve or thirteen years of age, dressed in colorful frocks, dancing to the Chinese music.

Andy and Jim got off the ship and talked to some of the children, who were delighted to try out the English they had learned.

After wandering around the shops on the pier they decided to visit a famous factory where the young women sat weaving carpets in silk and wool. The carpets were spread out over the floors of every department.

Andy had been anxious to buy a small Oriental rug for her den. They were extremely expensive back in the States, but cost only a fraction of the price here in China. As they meandered through the aisles she saw a beautiful silk carpet in blue, red, and off-white - the very colors she had been looking for.

"Oh, Jim!" she exclaimed. "How exquisite!" She hesitated. "Should I buy it?"

"Why not?" he asked. "Andy, if there's one thing I've learned it's not to lose out on an opportunity. When you see something you like, if you don't buy it then, chances are you won't see it anywhere else. Not exactly the same thing. We won't be back this way again. You've found what you want. Buy it while you can."

Andy looked gleeful, like a schoolgirl about to do something naughty. This was all the encouragement she needed. "I'll take this one," she told the man in attendance. "How much is it?" She reached in her purse for her wallet.

"Bargain," Jim said in an undertone. "They expect you to bargain."

"Oh." The price was so much lower than she had been quoted back home that she had been about to pay the price the man asked.

"I don't know," she told him. "How will I carry this?"

"The rug is small," the man told her. "We can fold it and put a handle on it. It won't be any trouble."

Andy hesitated again, caught up in the game of bargaining. She had never done this before. The price the man had quoted came to about two hundred and fifty dollars in American money. She turned to Jim.

He spoke a few words to the man in Chinese. The man nodded and made up the package for Andy to take with her. For only two hundred dollars she had the carpet she wanted. How perfect it would look in the den! She felt like a child who had been given a free lollypop.

Soon it was time to return to the ship and lunch.

There were many more ports to see. Indonesia, Singapore, Bali, and last of all Hong Kong with its great bargains. The ship would be in Bali for a few hours, and Andy and Jim donned their bathing suits for a swim.

Early the next day Andy was busy at the computer again.

One day, after working every spare moment for just short of two months, Andy realized that the novel was finished. It had gone much faster than she had anticipated. Jim's encouragement had inspired her and spurred her on.

As soon as she finished the editing, Jim showed her how to transfer the novel to a floppy disk. She couldn't wait to get home and buy her own computer. She smiled fondly at Jim, grateful for all the help he had given her.

Two copies of the whole novel were printed out, ready to take with her.

The Purser entered the room just as the last page was being printed. "How's it going?" he asked. "Did you find everything you need?"

"Yes, we're all set," Jim told him. "Thanks for all your help."

"It's all done!" Andy exclaimed. "I can't believe it! Now all I have to do is find a publisher who's interested. It will have to be someone who's willing to handle a brand new writer. I don't have a reputation yet, so it will take some doing. No one knows who I am."

"I have a suggestion," the Purser said. "On our last cruise there were a couple of people who had just broken away from the publishing company they were working for, and were starting their own company. They have a few things in the works, but they need more good material. Perhaps you'd like to try them. If they like what you've written, you could get in on the ground floor."

"Sounds too good to be true." Andy turned to Jim. "What do you think?"

"It's worth a shot. Do you have a name and address?" he asked the Purser.

"If you want to come to my office I'll be glad to give it to you right now."

Andy was thrilled. "I'll mail it the minute I get home!" she told Jim.

"Why wait?" he asked. "We'll go to the mailing room and get it ready to mail at the next port. We still have another month and a half of the cruise left. Maybe there'll be an answer waiting for you when you get home."

They soon had the name and address of the publisher in New York. It didn't take long to wrap up the novel for mailing. Andy kept the second copy and the floppy disk to pack in her suitcase.

She felt an excitement she hadn't felt since she married Paul. They were due to dock at the next port tomorrow morning, and her first novel was about to be mailed to a publisher.

Jim was just as excited as she was. Paul seemed far away.

CHAPTER VIII

It was evening, and Andy and Jim stood out on deck watching the moon dance on the water.

The cruise was almost over. The ship was scheduled to dock the next morning at seven-thirty.

Jim gazed tenderly at Andy. The past three months had brought them closer together than they had ever been. The look of love on Jim's face was unmistakable.

Andy stiffened, confused with what she was feeling. Before she could stop him, he reached out and took her in his arms.

At first she was surprised, but even more surprising was the fact that she didn't resist him. He lowered his lips to hers, and she didn't turn away.

He kissed her gently, then pulled her closer. The gentleness quickly turned into a deep passion. They were both swept up in an emotion so strong that neither one of them could fight it.

She responded with complete abandonment, overwhelmed with the desire that welled up in her. She had never felt this deeply toward Paul, and it frightened her. She found herself yearning for Jim to take her into his cabin and make mad, passionate love to her.

I mustn't let that happen, she thought. It wouldn't be fair to Jim. What if Paul comes back and we repair our marriage? Jim will just get hurt a second time. I can't do that to him.

She pulled away and turned her head.

Jim looked puzzled. "What's wrong, Andy?"

"This is," she replied. "This is all wrong. I'm being unfaithful. I should be thinking of Paul."

Jim interrupted her, indignation in his voice. "Was he thinking of you or me when he talked you into ditching me and eloping with him? He was thinking only of himself and what he wanted. He didn't care who he hurt in the process. He hurt not only me, but now he's hurt you. He's a very selfish man, Andy, and I think deep down you're beginning to realize it. In fact," he continued, "I think you're beginning to forget about him, and I'm glad. He's bad news, Andy."

"How can you say that?" she said, struggling with the conflict between her feelings for Jim, and what she was convinced was a betrayal of Paul. "He's my husband, and this is wrong!"

Jim all but exploded. "What kind of husband would desert his wife to run after other women and completely ignore all her years of loyalty? And on top of that, leave no address or telephone number where he could be reached in case she needed him? Wake up, Andy! You don't owe him a thing!"

Andy couldn't deny that there was truth in what Jim was saying, but she wasn't ready to admit it. She turned and fled back to her cabin in tears, brushing aside the hurt and disappointment she saw in Jim's eyes. He may hate me now, she reasoned, but he'll thank me later. I'd only end up hurting him again.

She rose at six-thirty the next morning, anxious to be among the first to go through customs. Her luggage was already in the lounge on the Promenade Deck, ready to be inspected.

After last night she couldn't face Jim with a clear conscience. She was trying hard to deny the feelings that his kiss had aroused in her.

The ship docked earlier than the scheduled time of seven-thirty. Andy was the first in line and got through customs very quickly, not stopping for breakfast. At seven-fifteen she hailed one of the cabs that was waiting outside and was soon on the ten mile drive to her home.

The first thing she checked was her answering machine.

No message from Paul.

She looked in his closet.

His clothes were still gone.

She went to the phone and called Midge.

Midge answered on the first ring. "Mom!" she exclaimed. "When did you get home?"

"I just walked through the door," Andy replied. "I checked the answering machine, and there's no message from your father. Did he call while I was gone?"

Midge's disgust came over the phone loud and clear as she answered her mother's question. "He called once. He said he tried several times to call you, but when there was no answer he finally called me. I knew he would. I told him you went on a trip. He wasn't upset. Just said that was good, he hoped you'd have a good time, and he'd stay in New York a while longer and check again."

Andy wasn't too surprised. But what stunned her was her lack of disappointment. To the contrary, she felt a great sense of relief. She needed this time to sort out her feelings. "I'm going to the Post Office to pick up the mail," she told Midge. "There's no food in the house. I'll have breakfast while I'm out. How about joining me?"

"Just tell me where," Midge answered. "I want to hear all about the cruise. Did you have a good time? What about Jim?"

"How about meeting me at the coffee shop around the corner from the Post Office?" Andy suggested, carefully avoiding the subject of Jim.

"Fine! Give me an hour. I have some exciting news to tell you."

While Andy waited for Midge to arrive, she shopped for food, and stopped in at an appliance store to buy the same kind of computer, printer, and word processor she had used on the ship. One of the salesmen helped her, and made arrangements for them to be delivered and set up later in the morning.

In slightly under an hour, Midge joined Andy at the coffee shop. "Hi!" She greeted her mother with a warm hug. "Boy, am I glad to see you!"

As soon as they were seated and had ordered, Midge scrutinized Andy's face. "Mom? You seem different - more mature - more your own person. You've changed. What's up?"

Andy smiled and ignored her remark. "What is this exciting news you wanted to tell me? It must be pretty important. I can tell by the expression on your face."

Midge was radiant. "Maybe you've already guessed! But I'm going to tell you, anyway! John and I are engaged! We want to get married before the end of the year. We plan to spend our honeymoon on the same ship you were on, and I want to hear all about it."

This was just what Andy needed to help get her mind off of her problems. "Oh, Midge!" she exclaimed excitedly. "What great news!"

"Mom, I'm so happy! John is wonderful!"

"I know he is," Andy agreed. "I'm glad you found someone so nice."

She gazed wistfully off in the distance. "Don't let anyone talk you out of it," she mumbled.

Midge changed the subject. "Have you looked at your mail yet?" she asked Andy.

"No. It's in the car. I've been shopping, and then I came right here to get something to eat."

Midge looked at her mother's plate. The food had hardly been touched. "Mom? Are you feeling all right?"

"Yes, dear, I'm fine. Just tired. Must be jet lag. We were in so many different time zones. I'm going home and get some rest if you don't mind." She rose from her seat and hugged Midge. "I'm so happy for you. John will make a wonderful husband and son-in-law. Be sure to tell him I'm delighted."

"Sure, Mom. Please - get some rest. Are you sure you don't want me to come back to the house with you for a while?"

Andy patted Midge's hand. "No, dear. I really need this time to myself to get caught up. I have to unpack and get the food into the house and put away. Then I'll look at the mail and go straight to bed. Don't worry about me. I'll call you in the morning."

Andy couldn't help noticing the look of concern in Midge's eyes as she drove off. Oh, dear, she thought, I'm not doing a very good job of covering up. She knows something's bothering me. She probably thinks it's because Paul hasn't come home yet, but I almost don't care if he does.

This revelation startled her, but it was true.

When she got home she was too tired and disturbed to do anything but put away the food and wait for the man to come with the computer. He arrived ten minutes after she walked through the door, and in less than an hour the computer and printer were plugged in, the word processing system was installed in the computer, her novel on the floppy disk was safely transferred to the machine, and everything was ready to use.

The minute the man left, Andy crawled into bed, too exhausted to look at the mail. She was soon fast asleep.

CHAPTER IX

Back on the ship it was seven in the morning when Jim woke up. He showered and dressed in a hurry, ready to have breakfast on deck and watch with Andy as they pulled into port. He left his cabin for the last time and knocked on Andy's door.

"Andy," he called, "they're serving pigs-in-a-blanket again. Are you ready to go up on deck and watch us come into port?"

No answer.

"Oink-oink," he chanted.

The door opened and a steward greeted him. "Yes, Sir, may I help you?"

Jim's smile faded. "Oh - I was looking for Mrs. Jordan. Is she here?"

"No, Sir, she already left," the steward informed him.

"Oh." Jim's heart pounded with disappointment. "What time did she leave?" he asked the steward.

"It was very early - I believe about six-thirty."

"She must have gone up to the deck already," Jim said, and turned to leave.

The steward stopped him. "Are you Mr. Rogers?"

"Yes."

"Just a moment, Sir." The steward disappeared inside the cabin. He returned with an envelope in his hand. "Mrs. Jordan asked me to give you this," he said.

Jim took the envelope from him and opened it.

"Dearest Jim," the note said. "Please forgive me for leaving without saying goodbye. I want you to know how much I enjoyed being with you, and how much I appreciate all your help and encouragement. I honestly don't think I could have made it through the past three months without you. I don't deserve all you've given me after the way I treated you years ago. You deserve someone better than me. You said there's a lot of living to be done, and I hope you find what you're looking for. God bless you. I wish you all the best. Thanks for everything." It was signed, "With deepest gratitude, Andy."

Jim thanked the steward and left in a hurry. He raced down the stairs as fast as his legs would carry him, hoping to find Andy before she left the ship.

He took a quick look in the dining room and out on the deck.

No Andy.

He was too late.

He went down to the lounge to wait for his name to be called to go through customs. No breakfast for him, either. He had lost his appetite.

As soon as he got through customs he left the ship and picked up his car from the parking lot. With a deep sigh he started the long drive home to Santa Barbara.

He felt sad - lonely - empty. "I love you, Andy," he murmured under his breath. "I never stopped loving you."

He knew why she deserted him this time. Just in case she and Paul should reconcile, she didn't want to cause him any more heartache. But this is precisely what she did by leaving the ship so abruptly.

Why does she feel she owes anything to that bastard? She's suffered enough at his hands. Why would she even consider going back to him, even if he wanted her? He never deserved her. She thinks I deserve the best? She is the best! When will she stop putting herself down? Paul has had thirty years to humiliate her, and ruin her self esteem, and he's done a thorough job. I couldn't undo it in three months.

An hour after leaving the ship he drove into the circular drive in front of his home, parked the car in the garage, and walked into his house.

It was cool and damp from the ocean breezes. He lit a fire in the fireplace of his den and sat staring out the window at the ocean. The sun sparkled across the waves as they tumbled into the shore.

He was in a quandary. Should he contact her and try to talk some sense into her, or should he wait for something that might never happen - namely, for her to contact him? He decided to call Midge and make sure Andy was all right.

The phone rang several times before Midge answered. "Hi!" She sounded breathless.

"Midge? It's Jim."

"Jim! I just got back from having breakfast with Mom. What happened with you two? Mom didn't tell me anything, and I didn't want to pry."

"It's a long story, Midge. Is she all right? She left the ship without saying goodbye - just a note."

"Jim, I'm sorry," she apologized. She sounded exasperated. "I don't know what's the matter with her. Why does she feel she owes Dad anything? I hope he never comes back. I don't feel guilty saying it. I've never loved him, and he's never loved me. Mom should wake up and realize he's never loved her, either. There's only one person in this world that he loves, and that's himself. I really hoped you and Mom would end up together." She sounded disappointed. "I can't think of anyone I'd rather have for a stepfather." She paused for a moment, then spoke bluntly. "I wish you were my real father instead of the one I got," she blurted out. "It's strange, but - "

"What's strange, Midge?"

"I felt a bond with you the minute I saw you walk into Mom's cabin on the ship. I can't explain it. I felt as though I'd known you all my life. It was like nothing I ever felt with Dad."

This touched Jim very deeply. At first he didn't know what to say. "Thank you, Midge," he said when he could finally speak. "That means a lot, coming from you. If I had ever had any children I would have wanted one just like you."

"Well, I mean it," Midge said with emphasis.

Jim sensed that she wanted to say something else. "Midge?" he asked. "What is it?"

"There's a favor I'd like to ask you." She was silent for a moment. "John and I became engaged since we saw you."

"Midge! That's wonderful. He's a fine man. When?"

"We're getting married before the end of the year, and I'd like nothing better than to have you walk me down the aisle and give me away."

This took Jim completely by surprise. "Why, Midge, how nice of you to ask me! But what about Paul? He's your real father. I would think you'd rather have him."

"I don't even want him to attend," Midge snorted. "No, Jim. I want you. Unless you'd rather not - "

"Nonsense!" Jim exclaimed. "I'd be honored. Does your mother know? Maybe she has other ideas."

"No, Mom doesn't know. It's my wedding, and I'm sure she'd agree if she knew how strongly I feel. But I'd just as soon you didn't mention this to her. I'll handle it my own way and in my own time. I've already asked her to be my Matron Of Honor. It's settled then? You'll give me away?"

"Absolutely!" he agreed. "I won't say anything to Andy. I doubt if I'll be talking to her before the wedding, anyway."

"Thanks, Jim. I appreciate that. Now my two favorite people will be taking part in John's and my wedding. This makes it complete. I'll let you know the exact date. I don't think it's necessary for you to attend the rehearsal. It's a simple thing for you to walk me down the aisle. Then you'll just sit in the pew reserved for my family."

A warm feeling swept over Jim. "Thank you, Midge, for including me in your family. You don't know how happy that makes me!"

He hung up, still wondering if he should call Andy. He reached for the phone, then changed his mind. Something told him this was not the right time.

CHAPTER X

It was six o'clock in the morning the day after Andy returned from the cruise. The birds were singing and the sun shone brightly on the pool out back.

Andy stood over the stove flipping pancakes and sausages that she bought yesterday. Pigs-in-a-blanket. It reminded her of Jim.

She couldn't get him out of her mind. She missed seeing him sitting across the table having breakfast with her, and she finally faced the fact that she was deeply in love with him.

Everything seemed crystal clear.

She hadn't thought of Paul for some time - not in that way.

This time there was no feeling of guilt - just remorse that she had left the ship so suddenly and pushed Jim out of her life. It was the worst thing she could have done. She was trying not to hurt him a second time, but that is precisely what she did. I must have hurt him deeply. How could I have been so blind? Right motive, wrong move.

She realized it was nothing but stubborn, headstrong pride that had kept her from admitting years ago that she had made a terrible mistake marrying Paul.

Midge was right. Paul did me a big favor, leaving me.

A tremendous feeling of relief swept over her, and she knew what she must do. She would file for divorce immediately.

She reached for the phone and made a ten-thirty appointment to see Richard Ingalls, their family lawyer. It's strange, she thought, how calm you feel when you know you've made the right decision. She felt free and relaxed for the first time in years.

She picked up the pile of mail she had been too tired to open last night. As she flipped through it she saw that one of the envelopes had the return address of the publisher she had sent her novel to over a month ago. Her fingers trembled as she opened it.

"Dear Author:" the note said. "Thank you for your recent submission. It's an interesting story, and well written. You'll be hearing from us soon about our decision." It was signed "Maddison Publications."

Andy was puzzled. Is this an acceptance or a polite rejection? Oh, I'll probably never hear from them again. Or maybe they're considering it. How I wish I could talk to Jim! He'd know. Forget it! He's done enough for you. I'll just have to wait and see.

She decided to call Midge and tell her about the divorce.

The phone rang several times. Finally - "Hello?" Midge sounded breathless. "Sorry, I was in the shower. Mom?"

"Yes, dear. I woke up early. I have something to tell you before you hear it from some other source."

"I know! I know!" Midge's excited voice came over the wire. "Jim called you. You're going to divorce Dad and marry him!"

There was no mistaking the eagerness in Midge's voice, and Andy could just picture her crossing her fingers as she used to do when she was a child and wanted something desperately. She hated to disappoint her. "I haven't heard from Jim, dear," she told her. "But you're half right. Are you sitting down?"

"Yes, Mom. What's this all about?"

"I have a ten-thirty appointment with Richard. I'm filing for divorce."

Midge cheered. "It's about time! You deserve better than what Dad handed you."

"Well, I finally came to my senses, and I wanted you to be the first to know. If your father should call, please don't say anything. Let Richard handle it. I only hope Paul doesn't give me any trouble. I'll see what Richard has to say before I start worrying about that."

"Richard may try to talk you out of it," Midge warned.

"Not if I can help it," Andy replied. "There's no way I'll change my mind. It's taken me a long time to reach this decision, but I have now, and nothing can change it. I have to run. I'll talk to you later."

She hung up and poured another cup of coffee as she opened the rest of her mail. As she read one of the letters she almost choked. It was from the bank informing her that some of the checks she had sent out before leaving on the cruise had been returned marked "Insufficient Funds."

How could this be? She grabbed her coat and purse and left early enough to stop at the bank before going to her appointment with Richard.

The teller greeted her with a smile. "Yes, Mrs. Jordan, what can I do for you?"

She handed him the letter. "What's this all about? There's plenty of money in Paul's and my account to cover these checks!"

The teller looked surprised. "That account was closed," he told her. "Mr. Jordan withdrew the balance four months ago."

Andy's heart pounded with dread. "What? Half a million dollars? There must be some mistake! How could he do that? Half of it belongs to me!"

"There's no mistake, Mrs. Jordan. He asked us to make out a check to him and close out the account."

Andy was furious. Now she would have to go into more of the money her Aunt Phoebe had given her. "I'll take care of the checks," she told the teller.

Bewildered and outraged, she turned and walked out of the bank. As she walked along in a daze toward the lawyer's office she remembered something her aunt had said - -

"I'll give you this money on one condition. Promise me you'll put it into a private account under your name only. Don't under any circumstances tell Paul that you have it."

Andy had felt guilty doing this, but she had kept her promise not to tell him. She did, however, make Paul the beneficiary.

Now she understood why her aunt had never trusted Paul. She shuddered, and hoped that Paul hadn't found out about her private account.

The receptionist ushered Andy into Richard's office as soon as she arrived.

He greeted her with a smile. "Andy, how nice to see you! What can I do for you?"

Andy sat down and looked at Richard. She had so much to tell him. Where should she start? What would he think when she told him she wanted to divorce Paul?

Richard and his wife used to make up a frequent foresome with them on dinner dates until they were divorced two years ago. Surely he would understand since he had been through this himself.

"Richard, I've decided to divorce Paul," she told him. "Please don't try to talk me out of it. I've made up my mind."

She was amazed to see his face break out in a grin. "Thank God!" he exclaimed. "I've been wondering when you'd come to your senses!"

Andy was stunned. "I don't understand."

Richard spoke to her gently. "Now I can tell you why I divorced my wife. Andy, she and Paul were having an affair. I found out about it and told her I'd forgive her if she'd break it off, but she refused. I didn't tell you because I didn't want to break your heart."

Andy looked at Richard with sympathy. "I'm so sorry," she said. "I had no idea."

"That's past history," he assured her. He started to say something else, then cleared his throat nervously.

Andy waited. "Richard? What is it? Is there something else?"

Richard rose from his chair and walked over to the window. He was silent for a moment. Then he turned and faced her. "You're not going to like this. Midge swore me to secrecy, but now I think you have a right to know. She came to me because she didn't want to hurt you." He sat down again. "I hate to break my promise to Midge," he said, "but I don't think it matters now, since you're divorcing Paul."

Andy gripped the arms of the chair and braced herself. "Go on," she said.

"When Midge was only sixteen, Paul came to her one day. He was drunk. You were out doing errands. He burst into her room when she was doing her homework. He - he - " Richard stopped.

"He what?" Andy demanded. She sat glued to her chair, waiting.

"Paul tried to molest Midge. She handled it very well, I thought. She kneed him in the groin and ran out of the house. After that, she made sure she was never alone with him again."

If Andy had been angry before, now she was outraged. "Why didn't you tell me? You shouldn't have waited all this time!"

"I think you know why I did. Midge didn't want to come between you and Paul. I told her she was making the wrong decision, but she said she could handle it. As soon as she was old enough she moved out of the house and into her own apartment."

Any doubt that may have been lurking in Andy's mind about divorcing

Paul, this and what she had just found out at the bank wiped it out for good.

"Tell me - what made you decide to divorce Paul?" Richard asked. "You didn't know about all this. There must have been some other reason."

Andy shook her head, still in a state of shock, trying to digest what Richard had just told her.

She rose from her chair and began to pace. "Three months ago Paul came to me and said he wanted to date other women, and wanted me to date other men. You know that's not my style. He went to New York, and I went on a round-the-world cruise to do some thinking. I returned yesterday. When I woke up this morning, I knew I had no choice but to divorce him. Now that you've told me this - " She was silent for a moment. Then she faced him with fury and determination. "How soon can we file for divorce?"

"I'll have my secretary draw up the papers right away. Where is Paul? Is he still in New York?"

"As far as I know. I have no idea where he's staying, but his company should know."

Richard nodded and dialed Paul's company. "Yes," he said when the receptionist answered, "where is Paul Jordan staying in New York?" He waited. "I see. Thank you," he said, and hung up. He was silent for a moment. Then he looked at Andy. "Did you know that Paul was fired from his job four months ago?"

"No! He never said a word!" How many more shocks were waiting for her? This was the fourth one today.

She was livid. Not only at Paul, but at herself for ever having trusted him. Anger that she had wasted all these years married to him, and anger that she had turned her back on Jim - twice. How could I have been such a fool? "Do you think Paul might try to fight the divorce?" she asked Richard.

"He'd better not!" Richard exclaimed. "You have plenty of grounds! Don't worry. I'll find out where he's staying, and as soon as you've signed the papers, I'll see to it that he's notified."

Andy's knees felt suddenly weak, and she sat down again. Her voice shook with anger. "Richard, there's something else. I just found out that Paul cleaned out our account at the bank several months ago. Half a million dollars. I have no idea where he or the money is."

"My God!" Richard exploded. "How could he do that to you? You didn't know until just now?"

"No." There was fear in Andy's eyes. "What has he done with it?"

"Don't worry," Richard assured her. "I know a good detective. I'll put him to work on this right away. Do you have enough cash to get along on in the meantime?"

"I have a private account - money my aunt gave me. It's up to somewhere around fifty thousand dollars. She made me promise not to tell Paul, and I didn't. But I made him the beneficiary. He's not entitled to it until I'm dead. With all the bills coming in, I have no choice but to use it. What if he finds out about it and tries to take that, too? I'm scared, Richard. It's all I have."

"There's no way he can touch it as long as it's not joint," Richard told her. "Keep it that way." He shook his head. "What was he thinking?"

Andy shrugged. "He loves the good life."

"We'll find the money he took and get you a good settlement on this divorce, I promise," Richard said, trying to allay her fears. "Was there anything else?"

"One other thing. I did something I've wanted to do for a long time. I finished writing a novel I started years ago."

Richard leaned forward in his chair. "Andy! That's great!"

"I sent it to a publisher over a month ago," Andy continued, "while I was still on the cruise."

"Who's the publisher?" Richard asked.

"Maddison Publications," Andy replied. "They're a new outfit. The Purser on the ship told me about them. They were looking for material. Here's a letter that was waiting for me when I got home." She handed it to him.

Richard took it out of the envelope and read it. "This looks encouraging. What do you know about this company?"

"Nothing except what the Purser told me."

"Let me look into this. You'll need a lawyer to handle it for you. If they're a reliable company they won't mind. They'll admire you for being so business like. It's for their security as well as yours."

He quickly jotted down the address and beamed. "It looks as though things might be looking up for you already. Let's hope they decide to publish your book."

CHAPTER XI

Three months went by and Andy heard nothing from Jim, Paul, or the publishing company. Richard's detective was working hard to locate Paul, but so far with no results.

Paul was using their credit card liberally, and the bills kept coming in to their Palos Verdes address. Since Andy still didn't know where he was, she had to pay them out of her own account. The money was dwindling at an alarming rate and she was getting desperate.

Richard's investigation into Maddison Publications checked out okay - the reputations of the two owners, Maddi Seaford and Sonny Dawson, were impeccable. But she couldn't wait any longer to hear from them. She had to do something to replenish her account, and she decided it was time to try other publishers.

She sat by the window and stared out at the ocean, trying to calm her nerves. She had just returned from the library where she obtained a list of publishers. She was so deep in thought, and her mind so eclipsed with worry, that she almost didn't hear the doorbell.

When she opened the door the postman handed her an Express Mail from Maddison Publications. Did she dare hope? She tugged at the tightly sealed envelope, and pulled out a letter and a document.

"Dear Mrs. Jordan:" it read. "We are pleased to inform you that we have decided to publish your novel. This is by far the best one that has been submitted to us. Please sign and Fax the enclosed contract, and keep this as your copy. As soon as we receive the signed contract, we'll wire you an advance check for ten thousand dollars. We plan to send you on a promotion tour as soon as the book comes off the press, and we need you in New York ASAP to finalize details. Please call and let us know when to expect you." It was signed, "Maddison Publications."

Andy whooped with joy, and whirled around the room in a wild dance. She grabbed the phone and dialed the publishing company. They told her they would make hotel reservations at the Park Plaza next to Central Park, and Maddi said she would meet her at Kennedy Airport.

As soon as Andy hung up she went into the room where Paul kept his Fax machine, and sent the signed contract to New York. She packed, ready to leave as soon as the check arrived. Next, she made an appointment with Richard. Then she dialed Midge to tell her the good news.

Midge answered on the second ring.

"Midge!" Andy was so excited she barely got the words out. "Hold on to your hat! Have I got news for you! I'm leaving on the one o'clock plane for New York."

"Oh, Mom!" Midge's voice showed her disapproval. "You're not going back to Dad, are you?"

Andy laughed. "No, dear. Nothing like that."

"Then why are you going to - ?"

"Midge," Andy interrupted, "I just received an Express Mail from a publishing company in New York. I did something on the cruise that I've been wanting to do for a long time." She smiled just thinking about it. "I finished a novel I started years ago. Jim helped me. He was wonderful. Your Dad always discouraged me, but Jim was so encouraging. If it hadn't been for him I doubt that I would ever have finished it. Four months ago while I was still on the cruise I sent it to a brand new publishing company - Maddison Publications. I just heard from them. They're going to publish my novel and send me on a tour to promote the book as soon as it comes off the press." There was silence on the other end. "Midge - Midge, are you still there?"

Midge screamed with delight. "Mom, that's great!! I always knew you could do it! Oh, this is super!" She paused as an unwelcome thought came to her. "You won't be seeing Dad, will you? He might try and talk you out of the divorce."

"I don't know his address," Andy reminded her. "There's no way I'll change my mind. Not after what he's done."

She paused for a moment. Should I say anything? she wondered. Yes. Midge should know. "Richard told me what Paul tried to do to you when you were only sixteen. You should have come to me."

Midge was silent for a moment. "I didn't want to cause any trouble."

"Honey, don't you know your safety and well being are the most important things to me?"

"Richard said I should tell you," Midge said. "I guess he was right. I had to turn to someone. I guess it should have been you. But I just couldn't."

"Never mind, dear. I understand," Andy assured her. "We won't have to worry about that any more. He's out of our lives." She looked at her watch. "I have to run. I have an appointment to see Richard. If you need me I'll be staying at the Park Plaza."

"You'll be back in time for my wedding, won't you? It wouldn't be a wedding without my Matron Of Honor."

"Honey, I wouldn't miss it. You know that. Even if I have to cancel one of my appearances." She laughed. "My appearances! Goodness, listen to me! I'm talking like a celebrity!"

"Mom - that's what you are! Get used to it! Just wait until Dad hears about this," she snorted. "I bet he'll come running back. You know how he loves the limelight. He'll probably try to upstage you and take all the glory!"

"I hope he doesn't give me any trouble about the divorce," Andy said. "I'm afraid he might if he hears about the book. I'll see what Richard has to say."

While she waited for the check to come she packed what she thought she would need. How does an author dress? she wondered. She had no idea how long she would be gone, or how much she should take.

She was so nervous thinking of all she had to do that her stomach was doing cartwheels. I need another cup of coffee to settle my nerves, she decided.

As she sat there trying to calm herself, the doorbell rang, and the check was in her hands. She took one final look around the house, set the answering machine and security alarm, picked up her suitcase, and left for her appointment with Richard. The receptionist ushered her into his office immediately when Andy told her she was on her way out of town.

"What's up, Andy?" Richard asked, eyeing her suitcase.

Andy was all smiles. "I'm on my way to New York."

Richard's eyebrows raised. "You haven't changed your mind about the divorce, have you?"

"No way!" she scoffed. "I have no idea where Paul is. He's the last person I want to see." She looked gleeful. "I've heard from Maddison

Publications. They've decided to publish my novel and they want me in New York! I'm booked on the one o'clock plane."

"No kidding!" he exclaimed. "Congratulations! Do you have any idea how difficult it is to get published? Most writers spend years trying. You're very fortunate!"

"I know. I got in on the ground floor. That's the only answer. They sent me an advance check for ten thousand dollars. I deposited it to my account on the way over here."

"What about the contract? Did they send you one? I'd like to look at it before you sign anything."

Andy looked startled. "Oh, I forgot! I guess I was so excited it slipped my mind. I signed it and Faxed it to them. They wouldn't send me the check until I did, and I needed the money. They said it was a standard contract."

"Well," Richard relented, "it's done now. God knows you can use the money. Paul pulled a rotten deal on you, making you pay all his extravagant bills."

Anger flared up again as Andy tried to control her feelings. "He's charging up a storm on our credit card," she told him. "I brought the latest statement with me so I can send the company a check from New York. I don't want any finance charges. It's a struggle just to pay the principle. You wouldn't believe how much money he's spent in such a short time. There'll be nothing left of my personal account if I don't put a stop to it."

Richard held out his hand. "May I see the statement?" he asked. He looked at the bill and shook his head. "If you don't mind I'll make a copy of this and give it to the detective. We might be able to track Paul down through one of the stores where he's been buying all these things."

"Anything that will help is okay with me," Andy told him.

He went into the next room and made a quick copy. In less than two minutes he returned and handed the original statement back to her. "Do you have enough money for your trip?" he asked. "I can lend you some if you don't."

"I have a thousand dollars with me and some travelers checks. That should tide me over for a while. I'll be staying at the Park Plaza. You can contact me there. I'd better get going," she said as she gathered up her purse and luggage. "It takes at least three quarters of an hour to drive to the airport, and it's almost noon."

"Let me drive you," Richard said. "I'm just about to leave the office, anyway." He rose from his desk before she could protest. "I'll get you there on time, don't worry," he promised. He picked up her luggage and steered her toward the door.

They arrived at the airport and Andy checked her baggage at curb side. She said goodbye to Richard, and entered the building. It didn't take her long to get through the security check and to the gate. She picked up her ticket and was soon comfortably settled in her seat on the plane.

In spite of her anger at Paul, she felt free and excited as she looked ahead. It was hard to believe that only three months ago she was on an ocean liner returning from a round-the-world cruise back to her quiet life. Now she was on her way to New York to settle details of her book that was about to be published. Her life had completely changed. She felt a sense of self-worth for the first time since she married Paul.

The five hour flight to New York was restful. She even nodded off once or twice. As they approached the airport she looked out the window. It was dusk, and the lights below twinkled like magic. She could see Long Island Sound as they banked to come in for the landing. The seat belt sign was on, and she made sure hers was securely fastened.

She had just one regret. Jim wasn't here to share it with her. I should let him know what's happened. I'd hate to have him find out through the newspapers. I'll send him a telegram as soon as I get to the hotel.

Should I ask him to join me? she wondered. No, I'll wait. Maybe he'll suggest it.

They taxied in to the gate, and she stepped out of the plane on to the ramp that led into the building. As she entered the airport, she saw a crowd of people waiting to greet their friends and loved ones.

One woman, very chic and attractive, was holding a sign with Andy's name on it. Andy guessed her to be in her mid-thirties. "Hi! I'm Andy Jordan," Andy said as she approached her.

The woman shook her hand warmly. "I'm Maddi Seaford. It's good to meet you. My associate, Sonny Dawson, is waiting at Sardi's Restaurant. I hope you're hungry. We want to take you to dinner."

Andy was surprised at the suggestion. "It's nine o'clock! Do people eat this late in New York? Won't the restaurant be closed by the time we get there?"

Maddi laughed. "Haven't you heard? New York is open all night. It never closes."

After picking up her luggage on the carousel, Andy followed Maddi to a waiting limousine just outside the door, and they were on their way to

Sardi's on Broadway. They stopped first at the Park Plaza and dropped off Andy's luggage, arriving at the restaurant well before the theatre crowd.

Andy was fascinated. She could feel the electricity of the atmosphere as she entered.

Maddi led her to a table where a pleasant looking man about Maddi's age greeted her with a big smile.

He rose when he saw them approaching, and extended his hand. "Andy!" he welcomed her. "I'd know you anywhere! You look just like your writing! Please," he gestured toward the seat side of him, "sit down. Let's get acquainted. I hope you're hungry."

Andy smiled. "Oh, yes, I can eat something. But not too much. I ate on the plane."

"That must have been hours ago." He motioned to the waiter. "Here," he said, handing her the menu, "they have light snacks if you don't want a full meal. And their cheesecake is to die for. You'll have to save room for that."

They had just ordered when the theatre crowd started to arrive. Soon the place was filled with wall to wall people, discussing the shows they just saw. The place was buzzing. As Andy looked around she saw some of the performers she had seen on the ship and felt she had entered another world - a fairy tale world, all sparkle and glitter - very much alive. She found it stimulating, and began to feel that she belonged.

"You don't know how surprised I was to get your letter," she told Maddi and Sonny. "I thought it usually took a lot longer with lots of rejections before an unknown writer could find a publisher who was willing to take a chance on a new author."

"That's true," Maddi agreed. "But the minute we saw your novel we knew we had a winner. It has just the right combination of pathos, excitement, intrigue, and mystery to hold the readers' interest. In fact," she smiled, "we're thinking of eventually making it into a movie-of-the-week for television."

"Really?" Andy was stunned.

"It has to become a best seller first," Sonny said, "and that's where you come in. As soon as it comes off the press we plan a publicity campaign that will make your novel take off with a bang! It will be great for our company if we can manage to get it off to a roaring start, and we think your novel has all the potential to do just that."

Andy felt a sense of unreality. Things like this didn't happen - not to her!

But this was real!

It was happening!

And why not? She had already wasted too much time allowing herself to be put down by Paul.

After an exciting two hours at Sardi's - being introduced to people she so far had seen only on television or in the movies - Maddi and Sonny led her out of the restaurant to the waiting limousine that would take her to her hotel.

As soon as she entered her room she sent a telegram to Jim.

When she woke the next morning, at first she didn't know where she was. Then she remembered, and excitement kicked in. She quickly showered and dressed, and went down to the restaurant just off the lobby to have breakfast.

As she entered, she was handed a newspaper, and ushered to a table that looked out on Central Park. Horse drawn carriages clip-clopped past the window, with happy tourists out for a morning ride through the Park.

In spite of the hustle and bustle of the city outside, it was peaceful and quiet in the restaurant.

Andy gave her order to the waiter and opened the newspaper. A flyer fell out, and Andy caught it before it reached the floor. It was a special section devoted to news about theatrical people and authors of books about to hit the bookstores.

As she started to put it back in its place she was startled by the headlines.

"New writer takes book stores by storm!" it read. "Andy Jordan's new novel is a knockout! It will be in the book stores by the first of the week, and it's a definite winner! Watch for 'The Clown Fell Down.' It's a sure bet! Don't miss it!"

As soon as she finished her breakfast, she approached the desk to see if Jim had answered her telegram. Her heart beat a little faster just thinking about it.

No message, the clerk told her.

Patience, she thought. He probably hasn't received it yet.

She went up to her room to prepare for whatever activities Maddi and Sonny had planned for the day.

CHAPTER XII

Jim had been home three months now with no word from Andy. It was early evening, and rather chilly. He lit a fire in the fireplace.

As he sat there he could swear he saw Andy's face leaping out of the flames. He couldn't get her out of his thoughts.

He decided to call Midge and see how Andy was doing. But just as he was about to dial her, the doorbell rang. It was a messenger with a telegram in his hand.

Jim gave the man a tip and opened it. It was from Andy.

What is she doing in New York? he wondered.

His heart sank. She didn't go back to Paul, did she?

As he read the contents of the telegram his whole face lit up. Andy's novel was being published! What wonderful news! "I have to talk to Midge!" he said, and reached for the phone.

Midge had just arrived home from her office. The phone was ringing as she entered the door. "Hello - Mom?" she asked.

"No, Midge, this is Jim. I just got a telegram from your mother. What wonderful news! I knew that novel was a winner!"

"Jim! Isn't it wonderful? She's a celebrity! Mom told me how much you helped her. She's very grateful to you, Jim. You did her a world of good! But what happened? She still hasn't told me anything."

"Oh, it's a long story, Midge. Has she heard from Paul?"

"Not a word," she told him. "Not since he called while she was on the cruise. I'm not surprised. I have some good news for you, Jim. Probably Mom didn't mention it to you in the telegram." She was so anxious to tell him that the words came tumbling out, falling all over each other. "Mom finally came to her senses. She saw a lawyer when she got home. Jim, she's divorcing Dad!"

Jim's heart skipped a beat. Could this mean - ? He didn't dare hope.

"She found out Dad was fired from his job four months ago, and never told her," Midge continued. "And he cleaned out their joint account at the bank - half a mil! And when she told the lawyer she wanted to divorce Dad, he told her why he divorced his wife two years ago. You're not going to believe this! Dad and the lawyer's wife were having an affair, and he found out about it! He kept quiet all this time, until Mom told him she wanted the divorce."

"So that's what finally made up her mind?"

"Oh, no. She'd already decided on the divorce the day after she got back from the cruise. Since then she's been paying all the bills that have come in. Dad's having a heyday charging everything to his and Mom's credit card. She had to go into her special account. She still doesn't know where he is, but the bills keep coming and have to be paid."

Jim was angry. "What is he thinking? He must know this is a terrible drain on her! Why doesn't he pay them out of the money he took from their account?"

"I don't know. Maybe he stashed it somewhere and he's hoarding it."

"Are you sure she's all right?"

"She's okay, but she misses you. She said it was because of you that she finally finished the novel, and she wished you were there to share it with her."

Jim didn't know what to say. He thought about going to New York and surprising Andy. No, he decided. I'll just send her a wire and let her know how thrilled I am that her novel is being published. Maybe she'll invite me to join her.

"Keep me posted, Midge," he said, and hung up.

CHAPTER XIII

Andy sat in her room at the Park Plaza deep in thought. It was six o'clock in the early evening, and the last of the sinking sun was about to disappear behind the brilliant sunset. The rosy glow that bounced off the tall buildings in colorful rainbow prisms seemed almost ethereal.

She had just emerged from a relaxing shower after an extremely busy day. Maddi and Sonny had kept her going at a dizzying pace, introducing her to so many celebrities and bigwigs in the publishing business, she couldn't remember half of their names. She was exhausted.

She missed Jim - more than she had ever missed anyone, including Paul. Especially Paul. She never dreamed she could miss anyone so much. If it hadn't been for Maddi and Sonny keeping her busy, she would have been hard put to survive the loneliness she felt at losing Jim.

She had been in New York for a month now. She had left instructions with the Palos Verdes Post Office to forward her mail, and the bills kept coming in.

She came to a sudden decision. Paul was draining her dry, and she had no choice. She picked up the phone and called the credit card company. "My credit card is lost," she told the person on the line. "Would you please issue a new one with only my name on it?" She gave them her Social Security number. "Thank you. Please mail it to the Park Plaza Hotel in New York." She hung up and cut her old card in half. Paul's access to the card was cancelled.

Her novel was due in the bookstores first thing tomorrow, and she was scheduled to appear at one in the heart of the city at nine o'clock sharp for her first book signing.

She hadn't heard from Jim since she sent him the telegram, and she was doing her best to put him out of her mind and just concentrate on her book. But it seemed like an empty triumph without him. He must have my telegram by now, she reasoned. Why haven't I heard?

There was a tap on her door, and she rose to answer it. "Yes? Who is it?" she called.

"Telegram," a male voice answered.

Her hopes rose. Jim?

She opened the door. The bellman had a telegram in his hand. She was so excited she almost forgot to tip him.

Her fingers shook with excitement as she opened it and pulled out the message.

It was very short. "I knew you could do it!" it said. "Congratulations! Keep me posted." It was signed, "As always, Jim."

Andy's eyes filled with tears as a deep sense of love swept over her. She wanted more than anything to call him and ask him to join her here in New York.

No, she decided, I've taken enough from him. I won't take any more.

With a deep sigh she put the telegram in her purse. This made her feel closer to him.

She reached in the closet for the designer suit she had bought at Bergdorf Goodman two days ago - a rich nutmeg brown with a jeweled collar and cuffs. To the suit she added a silk, beige blouse, the color of coffee after the cream is added. She threw her mink stole over her shoulders, picked up her jeweled purse, and left the room. Maddi and Sonny were due at six-fifteen to take her to dinner and a show. They wanted her to be seen in public as much as possible.

"We're having dinner at Chez D'Elegance," they told her as they ushered her out to the limousine. "It's a new French restaurant on Park Avenue."

"I've heard a lot about it," Andy said, trying to get into the spirit of a night out. She was determined to enjoy her new life, and not drop down into the deep chasm of regret that she felt.

Soon the limousine drove under the graceful porte-co-chere in front of the building. They entered the special elevator marked "Penthouse". Andy barely felt the rise as it left the ground floor and shot up.

In a matter of seconds they were on the sixty-fourth floor. It stopped just inside the restaurant. Crystal chandeliers hung from the ceiling and sparkled with a brilliance that reflected the lights from the skyscrapers seen through the windows of frameless glass. Andy felt like a princess in one of the fairy tales she used to read when she was a little girl.

Sonny stepped up to the podium and spoke to the maitre d'. "Maddison Publications," he said. "Party of three. We have a six-thirty reservation."

The maitre d' looked on the reservation sheet. "Oui, Monsieur. Right this way."

They followed the maitre d' across the floor. Down below, the cars and the people looked like busy ants parading. Andy could see for miles. The United Nations Building towered over the smaller apartment buildings, and beyond, the East River sparkled gaily in the moonlight.

As the maitre d' led them to their table by the window, Andy suddenly spied Paul. With him was a very young, strikingly beautiful woman. Andy guessed her to be a high fashion model.

Her first impulse was to turn and run. Richard had called her last night and told her that the detective had finally tracked him down. Does he know about the divorce yet? she wondered. Or the credit card? Either way it would be extremely awkward to have to face him right now.

Maddi looked in the direction where she was staring. "What's the matter, Andy? Someone you know?"

Andy put her hand up to hide her face. "I'm afraid so. I don't suppose we could go somewhere else?"

"We can try," Sonny said, "but I think most of the good restaurants are already booked. It's a popular night for the theater."

Andy made a quick decision. "Never mind," she said, gritting her teeth. "I'm not going to let him chase me out of here." She turned and looked out the corner of her eye, and could see that Paul hadn't noticed her. His table was across the room, and the maitre d' had seated her with her back to him.

"Are you okay?" Maddi asked.

Andy managed a shaky smile. "Yes, I'm fine!"

"I don't think whoever it is noticed you, if that's any consolation," Sonny told her.

"It's probably none of our business," Maddi offered, "but if we can help in any way - "

Andy interrupted her. "You might as well know. That man is my husband, Paul. I'm divorcing him. If he's received the papers from my lawyer he might cause a scene. I'd just as soon he didn't see me."

Sonny was sympathetic. "He seems quite engrossed with his companion. I wouldn't worry."

"I'm just grateful he doesn't read Variety - Billboard - Book Report - any of the theatrical newspapers," Andy said. "I have no idea how he may react when he finds out about the book."

"It might not be too late to go somewhere else if you really think it's necessary," Maddi told her. "We should be able to find a restaurant that could take us."

"No!" Andy assured her. "I have as much right to be here as he does!"

Sonny looked over in Paul's direction. "I think they're leaving," he told Andy. "Yes, they are. You can stop worrying."

"Thanks!" She grimaced. "He did everything he could to discourage me from writing," she explained. "I don't want him spoiling things now."

Maddi reached out and patted Andy's hand in sympathy and support. "Are you sure you're okay?" she asked.

"I'm okay now," Andy assured her. She shivered with dread as a sudden thought occurred to her. "I hope he's not going to the same theater that we are."

"Don't worry," Sonny chimed in. "You're safe with us. We'd better order if we want to get there on time."

As Andy reached for the menu she was startled when she heard a voice speak her name. She looked up and saw an actor and actress she had seen many times in soap operas.

The actor smiled and extended his hand. "Excuse me," he said, "but aren't you Andy Jordan? I understand your first novel is just out, and might be made into a movie-of-the-week. I hope you don't think I'm too bold, but is there a part in it for me? I'll be glad to audition for you."

"Yes," the actress echoed, "so would I."

Andy stared at them. She opened her mouth to say something, but didn't know how to answer.

Sonny quickly intervened. "We're not at that stage yet," he informed them. "When we are, notices will be put in Variety."

"Oh." The actor grabbed the actress' hand. "Nice to meet you," he said as they made a hasty retreat back to their table.

Andy was amused. Goodness, she thought, people I've admired for years asking me for a role in something I wrote? Unbelievable! She found herself regaining more of the self-esteem that Paul had robbed from her.

When they arrived at the theater, Andy took a quick look around, and breathed a sigh of relief when she didn't see Paul. He must have gone somewhere else, she guessed. But when the show broke for intermission, and they made their way to the lobby for some refreshing drinks, she saw Paul again with his stunning companion already at the bar.

Sonny took control. "Maddi, take Andy into the private room," he said. "I'll join you with the drinks. We'll be safe in there. Only celebrities and VIP's are allowed."

Maddi rushed Andy into the private room and the usher seated them at a small table. Sonny joined them, carrying three glasses of white wine. For the time being, Andy was safe.

"We'll wait until the last minute before going back to our seats," Maddi told her. "Don't worry about a thing."

They had fifteen minutes left, which gave them time to relax and enjoy their wine. Now all they had to be concerned about was keeping Paul from seeing Andy in the lobby afterwards.

While the actors were still taking their encore bows, Sonny steered Andy down to the lobby and into the limousine that waited outside the door.

Andy peered out the back window. Paul and his date were just exiting the theater. As they drove away she saw Paul staring at the limousine. Her heart pounded with dread.

"What's the matter, Andy?" Sonny asked. "Do you think Paul saw us?"

Andy's hands trembled. "I'm not sure. I hope not. The last thing I need is his appearance at the bookstore tomorrow." Her eyes filled with tears.

"Do you really think he'll cause a problem?" Maddi asked in a concerned voice.

"He'd better not!" Sonny was adamant. "Tomorrow is a very important day. I'd better be there just in case."

Andy was relieved. "Oh, would you? I'd feel a lot safer if you were. I hate to ask you - "

"You're not asking. I'm offering," Sonny interrupted. "It's important to our company to make sure nothing goes wrong."

They soon arrived at the Park Plaza. Andy said goodnight and went up to her room. She undressed and crawled into bed exhausted from dread. She had come this far. Nothing must interfere with her success. If only

Jim were here he'd know what to do, she sighed. Maddi and Sonny were doing a good job, but they weren't Jim.

She tossed and turned for half an hour, unable to relax enough to go to sleep. I need a good stiff drink. She looked in the private bar and found a bottle of brandy. She poured some into a glass and sipped it slowly.

She wasn't used to liquor. This is one of the things Paul used to chide her about. "Come on, Andy," he would say. "Get with it. Everybody drinks. Have a little fun."

Maybe he thought it was fun getting drunk and trying to molest Midge. She shuddered just thinking about it. However, she was grateful for the brandy tonight. It warmed her to her toes, and helped relax all the knots in her body. She crawled back into bed and fell asleep as soon as her head hit the pillow.

When she woke up the next morning, the first thing she remembered was what happened last night. Her stomach leaped to her throat, then took a roller coaster plunge.

It was six o'clock. She went into the bathroom and turned on the shower. The warm water was soothing to her tense body. She had just stepped out of the shower when her phone rang.

"All ready for the big day?" Sonny's voice came over the wire sounding happy and assuring.

"Just about," Andy replied. "Give me time to blow-dry my hair, put on my makeup, and dress - about fifteen minutes. Where are you?"

"Down in the lobby." Sonny paused. "You sound upset."

Andy's voice shook. "I have an awful feeling Paul is going to ruin everything."

"I don't see how he can, Andy. I think you've just got the jitters over your debut as a writer. Everything will be fine. I'll make sure of that. You get ready. I'll go into the restaurant and get a table. See you in a few minutes."

CHAPTER XIV

After Paul left the theater and dropped his date off, he went straight to his apartment house. The first thing he did was to go into the bar and order a straight whiskey. By now he had convinced himself that he was imagining things when he thought he saw Andy. What would she be doing in New York? he sneered. In a limousine? She's such a hayseed. New York and limousines are way out of her league.

He finished his drink and climbed the stairs to his dingy walk-up apartment. He hated where he was living now. This wasn't his style at all. It was a far cry from the posh suite at the Waldorf Astoria where he had been living since he left California four months ago. But he could no longer afford to stay there.

As he entered the apartment, he shuddered at the sparse furnishings, and cheap, ragged gauze curtains hanging at the windows. He had rented the place already furnished. Some of the upholstery was beginning to fray, and the garish colors were far from coordinated.

There was only one room and a bath. The tile was dingy, and needed a good scrubbing. The poor excuse for a picture window looked out on an alley, and all he could see was trash and wet, smelly garbage piled up, ready for the truck to pick up once a week.

A horrible place like this should be rent free! he fumed. I don't belong here. He couldn't wait to move out, but where would he go? It was all he could do to scrape enough together to pay the rent. And he wasn't ready to go back to California and his humdrum existence with Andy.

He had stashed the half a million dollars from his and Andy's joint account into a new account in a bank on the Cayman Islands, where no one could find it. But he couldn't touch that, as a minimum balance of five hundred thousand dollars was required to keep the account solvent. He had been living on the interest - not nearly enough to support his lavish life style. The $30,000 severance pay he received from his company was long gone.

He was shocked when they refused his credit card at the restaurant. Andy must have had it cancelled! he fumed. He was afraid she might, once the bills started coming in. He couldn't get a new card without proof of sufficient income, and he mustn't let the credit card company find out about his account in the Cayman Islands. Not only was it illegal, but they might notify Andy, and she would know where the money was.

With no way to charge anything, he had to do something to make some fast cash. If I get a job, he figured, it would have to be something special - something befitting my football star status. No nine to five job for me! But what? I can't get a reference from my last company. They fired me.

Too bad I don't have access to Andy's special account. I could use that until I get back on my feet. But she has to be dead before I can touch it.

He poured himself a Scotch from the bottle he kept beside his bed. He sipped his drink, and opened the newspaper he had bought that morning. Maybe I'll stumble across an opportunity I haven't thought of, he muttered to himself.

As he opened to the theater section, his eyes nearly popped out of his head! There was Andy's picture! Or was it Andy? The picture looked younger, more the way she looked when they first met. What has she done to her hair? It was shorter, and very attractive.

As he stared, he saw the headlines. "New Writer Hits Literary Scene With A Bang!" it said. He put his glass of Scotch down on the table and continued to read the article. Then he saw her name - Andy Jordan! Then it was Andy that I saw!

The article said the book was destined to become a best seller. Quick money! I've found it! The gold mine I've been looking for! The article further stated that she would be appearing at the Star Bookstore on Forty-Third Street tomorrow morning.

I'll go to see her and tell her how much I've missed her, and how sorry I am to have made such a terrible mistake in leaving her! Somehow I have to convince her I still love her. I won't let her become a millionaire without getting my cut! She's my wife, and community property says she owes me half! he declared, conveniently forgetting that the half million he deposited in the bank in the Cayman Islands was half hers.

He finished his Scotch and went to bed. When he woke up it was seven o'clock. He hopped out of bed, showered, shaved, and dressed, and went around the corner to the dingy coffee shop. All he could afford was the breakfast special - two dollars and ninety-five cents. The food was greasy, but it went down easier as he thought of what lay ahead if he could just get Andy to take him back.

As he ate he began to plot his strategy. He didn't want to leave New York and its sophisticated way of living. But California is nice, too, he reflected, as long as you know the right people. There'll be plenty of great parties, and with Andy on my arm, what attention I'll attract! With all the appearances she'll be making we'll probably get back to New York often - maybe even travel abroad!

He almost cheered out loud, thinking of the kind of life he'd be leading. He caught a glimpse of himself in the wall mirror. His hair was beginning to grey a little at the temples, but he was as handsome as ever. You've still got it! he exulted.

When he returned to his apartment it was time to leave for the bookstore. He sneaked a last look in the mirror and walked down to the street. No taxi for him. He had to go easy with the money he had left. Not for long! he promised himself. Things will be different soon.

The subway stopped just around the corner from the bookstore. Copies of Andy's book had just arrived, and Sonny was outside taking care of the delivery as Paul walked up. "Nice day," Sonny greeted him. "Are you here for an autographed copy of our latest book?"

Paul pulled himself up proudly and turned on the charm as he answered Sonny. "My wife wrote that book. I always knew she could do it. She's a very talented lady. I want to be by her side and give her all the support I can."

"Oh?" Sonny raised his eyebrows and gave him a piercing stare. "Does she know you're here?"

Paul hesitated. "Well - no. I'm here on a business trip. I want to surprise her. I've always encouraged her. It's about time the world knew how talented she is. I tried to tell her long ago to write, but she was so busy raising our beautiful daughter, she couldn't find the time. Our daughter, Midge, is a grown up lady now. She's our pride and joy, but I'm glad Andy finally came to her senses and started writing."

Sonny remained poker faced. "You didn't know about the book?"

"Oh, yes," Paul lied, "but I didn't know it would come out this soon. Andy probably didn't want to interfere with my business meetings, so she kept quiet. I read about it in the paper this morning." Paul thought he had Sonny fooled with his phony charm.

"I think if you come back around four o'clock it might be better," Sonny suggested with a smile. "Andy will be swamped with wall to wall people wanting her to autograph her book. You know how it is."

This appealed to Paul's ego. "Oh, yes! I've had to sign my share of autographs in my day. I was Captain of the football team in college, you know - constantly surrounded by adoring fans," he bragged. He paused, thinking. "Maybe it would be better if I went to her hotel later."

"Whatever you think," Sonny agreed. He went back into the store, and Paul left.

He no sooner arrived back at his apartment when there was a knock on the door. A man stood there with an envelope in his hand. "Are you Paul Jordan?" he asked him.

"Yes, I am," Paul replied.

The man handed him the envelope. "This is for you," he said, and left.

Paul went back inside the apartment and opened the envelope. The divorce papers fell out. When he reached down and picked them up, at first he thought he was seeing things. He never believed that Andy would have the gumption.

"She can't do this to me!" he exclaimed out loud. "Well! I guess two can play this game! She'll be sorry she ever started this! So Richard is handling it, is he? He's just trying to get even with me for carrying on with his wife! We'll see about that!"

He grabbed the newspaper with Andy's picture and was about to throw it away when he saw an ad that caught his attention. It was outlined in a bold, wide border. Why hadn't he noticed it this morning?

"Interesting offer for gentleman who qualifies," it read. "Free rent in exchange for the right person to take care of Park Avenue condo for a year." It gave the address and phone number of a realtor.

Paul reached for the phone and dialed the number. "I saw your ad in the paper," he said when the man answered. "I have just the qualifications you're looking for."

"What is your name?" the realtor asked.

"Paul Jordan. I'm Andy Jordan's husband. You know - the author."

"Oh!" the realtor exclaimed.

Paul could tell that the man was duly impressed.

"When can you come to the office?" the realtor asked him. "This must be taken care of today."

"I can be there in twenty minutes," Paul told him.

He hung up and put on his best suit before going down to the street. No more subways for me! he crowed. This time he hailed a cab. I can afford it now! No more rent to eat up my cash! When he arrived, the realtor and another man were waiting.

"Mr. Jordan," the realtor said, "meet David Springer. He's leaving for Europe tonight for a year, and doesn't want to leave his condo empty. He's looking for a man who's honest, neat, and dependable to stay there while he's away. Do you think you can handle it?"

"I certainly can!" Paul exclaimed. "You can trust me. I'll keep the place as if it were my own."

David Springer smiled. "I understand Andy Jordan is your wife. I've read her book. She's a very talented lady. I'll be proud to have you stay in my apartment. When can you move in?"

"Right away," Paul replied. The sooner, the better, he mused. I can't get out of that hell hole of an apartment where I've been living fast enough!

The deal was closed in half an hour. Paul was given a key, and was back in his dingy apartment in another twenty minutes. He packed his scant belongings with lightning speed.

As he did so he noticed that his wardrobe was beginning to look shabby. Never mind, he thought. I can afford new clothes now with no rent to pay. He picked up his luggage, and went outside to hail a cab.

By the time he arrived at the apartment on Park Avenue, David Springer had gone.

After depositing his things in his new apartment, Paul went to Bloomingdale's. Before long he had run up a tab of several thousand dollars. Nothing but the best for him.

He asked that everything be delivered to his new condo. The impressive address, and the fact that he was Andy Jordan's husband, gave him all the clout he needed. By the time the bill comes in, he figured, I'll have my credit card back and plenty of money. All I have to do is mention Andy's name.

Life was rosy once more.

CHAPTER XV

At the bookstore an excited Andy was busy signing autographs. The hours rolled by. No time for lunch.

It was five o'clock, and by this time Maddi had joined them. "How did it go?" she asked Andy.

"Great!" Andy replied. "But I never dreamed how tiring this could be!"

Maddi nodded. "Well, brace yourself!" she told her. "I've set you up for a television interview tomorrow afternoon. Let's get something to eat. I know it's early, but you must be starved. We'll get a snack at the Waldorf Astoria coffee shop," she said as they got into the limousine.

As they entered the lobby of the hotel Andy was deeply impressed with the simple but rich elegance of the decor. The walls were covered with elegant wallpaper, and the luxurious upholstered chairs and sofas added an Old World elegance. It reminded her of some of the places she and Jim had visited on their cruise. She quickly shook off the nostalgia.

They were led to a secluded booth in a corner of the coffee shop where they could talk in private. As soon as they were seated and had ordered, Andy faced them and grimaced. "I guess there's no way to keep this secret from Paul," she said.

"He already knows," Sonny informed her. "He came to the store this morning. I talked him out of coming in. I thought it was best not to mention it to you at the time."

Andy looked at him with gratitude. "Thanks, Sonny. I really appreciate that."

Sonny hesitated. "There's something else. Evidently he knows where you're staying. He plans to go to your hotel tonight."

Andy stiffened. "Well, I suppose I have to face him sometime."

"Don't let him do a snow job on you," Sonny warned. "I know he's your husband, but he's a real con artist. He tried to tell me he'd always encouraged you to write, and the reason you didn't was because you were busy raising your daughter. He said, 'Midge is our pride and joy, but when she became an adult I finally persuaded Andy to start writing.' I had a hard time not to laugh in his face."

"What a liar he is!" Andy exploded. "Paul is the one who stopped me! Every time I tried, he found a way to drag me away from it. It was only when I went on a cruise and was reunited with the man I was engaged to before I married Paul, that I found the encouragement I needed. Jim was wonderful." She spoke in almost a whisper. "I should have married him instead of Paul."

Maddi gave her a searching look. "I think you're still in love with this man."

Andy sighed. "It took the cruise to wake me up. But after the way I treated him years ago I can't expect him to take a chance with me again. It wouldn't be fair."

"Sounds like a plot in a novel," Sonny observed. "Maybe this could be your next one."

Andy managed a faint smile. "Unfortunately, it's all too true. Jim should be here with me. He's so much a part of my success. Paul made me feel like an idiot. You have no idea - " Her voice broke and trailed off as she struggled for composure.

"That's why you're divorcing him?" Maddi asked.

"That, and other things."

"How does your daughter - Midge, is it? - feel about it?" Sonny asked. "The divorce, I mean?"

Andy snorted. "Midge cheered when I told her."

"How does she feel about Jim?" Maddi queried.

Andy's eyes grew warm. "She's the one who made sure we were on the same cruise. She'd like nothing better than for me to marry him as soon as the divorce from Paul is final."

"Jim never married?" Sonny asked.

"Oh, yes. His wife left him and stayed in France. Their divorce is probably final by now."

"I think you two belong together," Maddi told her.

Andy looked wistful. "I sent a telegram to Jim and told him about the book being published. I felt he had a right to know. He sent me a telegram congratulating me."

"Sounds as though he still cares," Maddi said. "Maybe you two will get back together again."

Andy shrugged. "I doubt it."

They finished their tea and snack, and headed back to the Park Plaza, deciding to skip dinner and get to bed early.

"Why don't you tell the clerk you don't want to be disturbed," Sonny suggested. "If Paul does come, you won't have to see him."

"Thanks, Sonny," Andy replied. "I'll do that."

After speaking to the clerk Andy walked to the elevator and went up to her room. She was looking forward to a warm shower, a brandy to relax her, and a good night's sleep. But when she looked in the private bar there was no brandy. The maid must have forgotten to replace it, she figured. She picked up the phone and ordered some from Room Service.

CHAPTER XVI

Paul sat in his new, posh condo mulling over the situation. How was he going to talk Andy out of divorcing him? He was determined not to let his newly found gold mine slip away.

It was almost six-thirty in the evening. He poured himself a straight Scotch and turned on the television news. As he watched, he saw a limousine pull up in front of the Park Plaza Hotel. Camera men were lined up on the sidewalk, and Andy got out. Maddi and Sonny were with her.

"So!" Paul said out loud. "She's back at the hotel. I'd better get over there."

He finished his glass of Scotch, donned his jacket, and left. The doorman hailed a cab for him, and he was on his way. Traffic was heavy, and he became impatient. Now that he had decided what he was going to do he was anxious to put his plan in motion.

Maddi and Sonny were still there when he finally arrived. The photographers were just leaving. Great publicity! Paul mused. Soon I'll be part of it! He hid outside the hotel where he couldn't be seen and waited until Maddi and Sonny left in the limousine. Then he entered the hotel and approached the desk.

"Good evening. I'd like Andy Jordan's room number, please."

"Oh, I'm sorry, Sir," the clerk replied, "but Mrs. Jordan left strict orders not to be disturbed."

Paul smiled with all the charm he could muster. "I'm her husband."

The clerk hesitated. "I'm sorry, Mr. Jordan. I have strict orders."

"But I'm her husband," Paul insisted. "She didn't mean me."

"Just a moment, Sir." The clerk picked up the phone and pressed the buttons for the number of Andy's room.

Paul watched to see what numbers he was pressing.

"Mrs. Jordan, your husband is here," he heard the clerk say. "Yes, Mrs. Jordan, I'll tell him." He hung up and addressed Paul. "Sir, your wife said she's retired for the night."

Paul walked to the other side of the lobby and waited until he was sure the clerk wouldn't see him. Five minutes - ten minutes - fifteen minutes.

Finally someone else approached the desk. The minute the clerk's back was turned, Paul sped to the elevator. He pushed the button for the sixth floor. Andy's room was only a few doors down the hall.

Paul knocked.

Andy called through the door. "Just leave the brandy outside, please. Thank you."

Paul waited, not making a sound.

In a couple of minutes Andy opened the door, dressed in her robe.

Paul stood there all smiles. "Hi." He greeted her as though the past few months had never happened. "It's good to see you." She tried to close the door, but he pushed his way in. As he entered he held up the divorce papers, a hurt look on his face. "What's this all about, Andy?"

Andy closed the door and faced him. "It's just what it looks like. I'm suing you for divorce."

Paul assumed his most innocent expression. "Why? We need to talk, Andy. Look, I'm terribly sorry for putting you through all this. I made a big mistake. Middle age crisis. I still love you, and I want you back. We can work things out."

Andy sighed. "Paul, whatever you have to say you can say to Richard. Didn't the clerk tell you I didn't want to be disturbed?" This wasn't at all what Paul had expected. "Please, Andy," he pleaded, "I said I was sorry. I made a mistake. I want you back."

"For how long, Paul? Until the next time you get bored?"

Paul decided to try another tactic. "Oh! I get it! Now that you're a famous writer you want to leave me."

Andy laughed out loud. "I think you're the one who left me, Paul."

"But I never wanted a divorce. Just my freedom to have some fun. We were in a rut."

Andy stared at him. "YOU never wanted a divorce. YOU just wanted your freedom to come and go as YOU pleased. Why is it always what YOU want, Paul? What about what I want? Or doesn't that matter to you?"

Paul hesitated, then decided his best line of attack was to put the blame on her. "Have you been carrying on behind my back? Is there someone else?"

Andy surprised him with her direct answer. "Yes, Paul, there is. I'm in love with someone else."

An angry look crossed Paul's face. His gold mine was slipping away. "Who is this guy who wants to steal my wife?" he demanded.

Andy whirled around and confronted him. "The way you stole Jim Roger's fiance a week before the wedding? Look who's talking! Paul - really!"

Paul continued to blame her for everything that happened in the past few months. "Is it someone you met on the cruise? Is it Jim? Was he on the cruise?" He knew by her silence that he had guessed right. "Did you two plan to go together on the cruise? How could you do this to me?"

Andy waited until he stopped shouting. "I'm sorry, Paul, but this is the way it is, and it's not going to change. And to answer your question - yes, I'm in love with Jim, and yes, we were on the same cruise. But we didn't plan it. Midge did. I didn't know he'd be there until I boarded the ship."

Paul turned red with anger. "Midge? How could she? You turned her against me!"

Andy snorted. "Paul, she's not stupid. She's known for years what's been going on."

"I'll fight this, Andy. You have no grounds for divorce."

Andy gave him an icy stare. "You deserted me, Paul."

"I had every intention of coming back! What's happened to you? You've changed!"

"Yes, I've changed," she snapped. "Does that surprise you? This sometimes happens when a husband deserts his wife to chase after other women. It's quite an eye opener. Now please go. We have nothing further to say."

Paul tried desperately to think of something that would put their marriage back together. "What about Midge? I'm her father. I have some rights. She'll be devastated if we divorce."

Andy snorted. "Believe me, Paul, she's delighted. Since when did you ever act like her father? You never paid one iota of attention to her from the day she was born! Except for the time you tried to molest her. Did you think that was one of your so-called rights? How could you, Paul?"

"I never molested Midge! How could she say I did?"

"She didn't," Andy replied. "Richard told me."

"Richard! You mean she went to him?"

Andy glared at him. "She had to talk to someone and she didn't want to tell me. She was afraid it would hurt me. But I wish she had. I would have left you long ago."

"She's lying!" Paul shouted. "I never touched her!"

"Only because she wouldn't let you!"

Paul walked over to the window and looked out. Then he turned around and spoke to her, putting her down the way he always did to get his way. "So you're in love with Jim, are you? Surely you don't think he's in love with you! Can't you see he's just trying to even the score by stealing you away from me? As soon as he succeeds, he'll drop you so fast you won't know what happened. And you fell for it! How could you be so stupid?"

Andy didn't answer, and Paul realized his old tricks weren't working.

There was a knock on the door. The brandy that Andy ordered had arrived. She held the door open as she turned and spoke to Paul with maddening calm. "Paul, I want you to leave. Now!"

"You haven't heard the end of this!" Paul threatened. "I'll sue you for my half of community property!"

Andy gave him a cold stare. Ice could have fallen from her lips as she answered him. "Fine! And I'll sue you for my half of the five hundred thousand dollars you took from our joint bank account when you closed it without telling me, leaving me to pay all your ridiculous bills!"

"What else could I do when you had my credit card canceled?" he shouted.

"Paul! Really! You made all those huge charges long before your card was canceled! Now please go before I lose my temper!"

"Well - " he floundered - "you have a nice, private bank account you can use! When were you going to tell me about that?"

"I made you the beneficiary," Andy told him.

"You made sure I couldn't touch it until you're dead! What good is that?" He reached into his pocket and pulled out a card with his Park Avenue address and phone number, and put it on the bureau. "This is where I'm staying in case you change your mind about the divorce," he told her.

He walked through the open door and left.

CHAPTER XVII

Andy stood in the doorway of her hotel room clutching the bottle of brandy. She watched Paul strut down the corridor toward the elevator. How could I have been married to such a jerk for thirty years and not known how self-centered and selfish he is? she marveled.

His threats rang in her ears. In spite of her newly acquired bravado where he was concerned, she was filled with fear. Could he possibly fight the divorce? Or worse still, get half of my royalties? That wouldn't be fair! Not after the way he always discouraged me! Not after cleaning out our account and leaving me to pay his horrendous bills with what Aunt Phoebe left me. He owes me, not the other way around!

His words haunted her - "Jim doesn't love you. He's just trying to get even with me!" This played over and over in her mind like a broken record. Could that be true? "No, Jim isn't like that!" she declared out loud.

As soon as she saw Paul enter the elevator, she closed the door and double locked it. She shook with anger as she poured some of the brandy into a glass and chug-a-lugged. She choked. Paul is enough to drive anyone to drink! she thought as she struggled for breath.

The brandy bit her throat as it went down, but helped to calm her nerves once she stopped choking. Then she picked up the phone and called Richard.

"What's up, Andy?" he asked. "You sound upset."

"Paul was just here," she told him. "He threatens to fight the divorce. He wants a huge settlement. He mentioned community property. And he knows about my special account. He can't get half of what I make with my writing, can he?"

Richard laughed. "Andy," he assured her, "he doesn't stand a chance. He not only deserted you - he didn't even tell you where he was staying or where he stashed the half a million dollars. He'd be laughed out of court. He's just trying to bully you."

"Oh," Andy sighed, "thank you, Richard. What would I do without you?"

"You just concentrate on your book. I'll take care of this."

Relieved, Andy hung up and crawled into bed.

For the next week she was busy signing books and appearing on talk shows.

One evening she was dining alone in the restaurant just off the lobby of the hotel when she heard herself being paged.

"Andora Jordan. Phone call for Andora Jordan."

She summoned the waiter. "Would you please bring me a phone?" The waiter was back in two minutes with the phone.

The call was from Midge. "Are you almost through autographing books?" she asked. "John and I have set a date. We're getting married in two weeks. I hate to pull you away from New York, but I need you here."

"You couldn't keep me away!" Andy exclaimed. "I'll tell Maddi and Sonny I have to get back to California. They'll understand. I'll take the noon plane tomorrow."

"You're sure I'm not dragging you away?" Midge asked.

"No," Andy replied. "I'd like to get away from here for a while, anyway. I need a respite. This pace is hectic."

"Great! I've missed you. Do you know what time the plane gets in?"

"With the time difference I would say sometime on or about two o'clock."

"I'll check with the airline and meet you at the airport. I'm on my way out now. John and I are driving up the coast to Ventura for dinner with some friends. I won't be back until late, but you can leave a message on my machine. See you tomorrow," Midge said, and hung up.

As soon as Andy finished dinner, she went up to her room and dialed Maddi. "I just got a call from my daughter," she told her. "She's getting married in two weeks. Can you spare me for a while?"

"Oh, sure," Maddi agreed. "Is there anything I can do?"

"Just come to the wedding. Tell Sonny."

"We wouldn't miss it!" Maddi replied.

"Good! I'll be in touch with details. You'll stay at my home, of course. Talk to you later."

She was tired, and decided to get a good night's sleep, ready for the long trip to California tomorrow.

She was sound asleep when the phone rang. She looked at her watch on the night stand. Eleven o'clock. Who can this be? she wondered.

It was John. He was extremely upset. "Andy," he said, "I hate to tell you this, but you'd better get here as fast as you can. I'm calling from the hospital in Ventura. There's been a terrible accident. Midge is badly hurt. She's lost a lot of blood and needs a transfusion. She has a very rare blood type, and the blood bank is all out of it. I checked your type, and it won't do. We'll need Paul. Do you know where he is?"

Andy held on to the phone table to keep from fainting. "Yes, John, I'll get hold of him right away. How bad is it?"

"Just get Paul here as fast as you can. You'd better take the Red Eye."

"Yes, John. What hospital is she in?"

"Memorial Hospital in Ventura," John told her.

She reached for the card Paul had left on the bureau. Please be in, she prayed as she dialed the number.

The phone rang several times before he answered.

"Paul," she sobbed, "Midge has been in an accident. She needs a transfusion, and I don't match. I'm taking the Red Eye back to California tonight. It leaves in an hour. Don't let me down. Midge needs you."

"Which airline?" he asked. "Got it," he said and hung up.

Andy phoned the desk. "I'm checking out," she told the clerk. "I don't know for how long. Please put my things in storage until I return."

She dressed in a hurry, threw a few things into a tote bag, and ran out the door. It seemed like an eternity before the elevator reached the lobby. "Please get me a taxi. I have to get to the airport." Her voice sounded calm, but inside she was churning.

The taxi sped through the streets of New York. Traffic wasn't heavy at this time of night, and Paul arrived at the airport the same time as Andy. He hopped out of the cab, grabbed both tote bags, and they entered the terminal together. The plane was fully booked, and they were put on a waiting list.

"Please!" Andy told the ticket agent. "This is an emergency!"

"We'll do what we can," the agent promised.

They had just sat down when the announcement came for them to approach the desk.

"We have two seats available in First Class," the clerk told them.

They sped down the electric walkway and were ushered to their seats just as the door closed. They were soon airborne on their way to California. Andy felt that she was running a race she couldn't win as she tried mentally to urge the plane to fly faster.

"They're flying as fast as they can." Paul sounded a little impatient. "She's my daughter, too,"

Andy looked at him in disbelief. What a hypocrite he is, she thought. He's probably doing this hoping I'll change my mind about the divorce. Never mind. He's here ready to help Midge. That's what matters.

It was two AM, California time, when they arrived at the Los Angeles Airport. Andy and Paul were the first ones off the plane. They hurried outside to hail a cab, but none of the cab drivers wanted to take them all the way to Ventura.

Andy rushed over to the starter. When she told him how urgent it was, he called a limousine on his cellular phone. The traffic seemed to part and make way for the VIP limousine as it sped over the freeway toward Ventura.

John greeted them in the lobby looking very worried. His arm was in a sling, and there were some bruises on his forehead.

"We got here as fast as we could," Andy told him. "How is she?"

"She's still with us," John informed them, "but she's very weak. She lost a lot of blood - too much. The glass from the windshield cut into an artery. Paul, please come with me. We have to double check and make sure you're a match."

Andy watched as they disappeared down the corridor.

In about ten minutes they reappeared looking grim.

Andy knew something wasn't right. She rushed up to John. "Is Midge all right?"

John nodded, but Andy saw a puzzled look on his face. What's wrong? she wondered.

John took her aside. "Andy, is there something you're not telling me? Midge has a very rare blood type, and Paul isn't a match, either." He waited for an explanation.

Andy was stunned. "What? Why?"

John hesitated, then came right to the point. "Is Paul Midge's real father?"

Andy sat down, unable to stand. "Of course he is!" she declared. What is going on? Time is wasting, and Midge needs help.

Suddenly she gasped. "Oh - it can't be!"

"Andy - what is it?" John asked her.

She stared at him, for a moment unable to utter a sound as the truth dawned on her. Never in all the years she had been married to Paul had she suspected this.

She remembered the one time she and Jim had come together. It was two weeks before their wedding was supposed to have taken place, and just before she met Paul. One night they drove to the lake. The air was balmy with the first touch of spring, and the moon shone on the water with a golden glow. They were carried away with the breathtaking beauty.

Jim whispered in her ear. "We'll be married in a couple of weeks. Why wait?"

Andy had been as eager as he was. Before they knew it they were swept away on a sea of emotion. She remembered it vividly as the truth came flooding back.

No wonder I became pregnant so soon after I married Paul! she thought. I must have already been pregnant! Jim must be Midge's real father!

She ran to the phone and dialed Santa Barbara.

"Hello?" she heard on the other end.

"Jim," she sobbed, "it's Andy. Thank God you're there. I'm calling from Memorial Hospital in Ventura. Can you come here right away? Please hurry! Midge has had an accident and needs a transfusion. I can't explain now, but I think you may be a match. Please come!"

Jim didn't wait for an explanation. "I'm on my way," he said.

Andy hung up in a daze and returned to the waiting room.

John came over to her immediately. "What's going on, Andy? Do you know someone who can help Midge?"

"Yes," Andy replied. "Jim is on his way. He'll be here in an hour."

Paul, sitting across the room, rose and came toward them, an accusing look on his face. "Is there something you haven't told me?" he asked angrily.

Andy was in no mood for his accusations. "Please, Paul. Now is not the time. Midge is in there fighting for her life."

"I'm not her father, am I? All these years I've been loving her, thinking she was my daughter, and she's not. How could you do this to me?"

Andy exploded. "Since when have you ever loved Midge? I didn't know about this, Paul. Do you think I would have hauled you all the way from New York if I'd known? I'm just as surprised as you are."

Paul spoke to her with anger, but with a tinge of triumph. "I'm going back to New York and see my lawyer. I guess now I have grounds to fight this divorce and get a nice settlement." He marched out of the hospital, not waiting to find out if Midge was going to recover.

Andy was too worried to care what Paul thought or did. She and John waited nervously for Jim to arrive.

"How did the accident happen?" she asked John.

John sounded angry and bitter as he answered her question. "A police chase," he said. "The driver had just come off the freeway, and a police officer was chasing him. We were crossing an intersection when he appeared out of nowhere and slammed into us. They have him in custody. He wasn't hurt. Midge took the worst of it. If I ever get my hands on him - " his voice broke.

Andy looked anxiously at her watch just as Jim walked into the waiting room. He arrived in half an hour. He must have driven like a demon, she thought.

She rushed over to him. "Jim," she sobbed, "I can't take the time to explain. Please go with John. He needs to test your blood type. Midge has lost a lot of blood and she needs a transfusion. Yours should match."

Jim went immediately with John. In about fifteen minutes John returned looking relieved. "He's a match," he told Andy. "He's in the emergency room with Midge. They're prepping him for the transfusion."

Andy collapsed on the sofa. John sat down and took her shaking body in his arms. "It's okay," he said soothingly. "There's a good chance now that Midge will make it."

Andy spoke between sobs. "I should explain - "

"Hush," John said. "There's no need. You didn't know Jim was Midge's father. It's too bad Paul didn't believe you. I hope he doesn't give you any trouble over the divorce."

"I don't care," Andy declared. "As long as Midge is all right, that's all that matters. Let him sue me."

Half an hour passed, and one of the doctors approached them. "The transfusion is over," he told them. "She's stabilized and her color has returned. You can see the patient as soon as she's had a little rest. She has some cracked ribs which will take some time to heal, but otherwise we expect her to make a full recovery now that the blood has been replenished."

"Where's Jim Rogers?" Andy asked. "I want to thank him." She glanced up as Jim appeared in the doorway looking pale and deeply disturbed. She rose to her feet and rushed over to him. "Jim - how can I ever thank you? You saved Midge's life!"

He looked at her coldly, an expression of disbelief and distrust in his eyes.

She recoiled. "Jim - I'm sorry. I didn't know - "

He turned on his heel and left the room.

Andy was shaking as she turned to John. "I didn't know - "

John nodded. "I know you didn't, Andy."

"First Paul - now Jim," Andy sobbed. "Why won't they believe me? I've got to find Jim and explain."

She ran out of the room and down the corridor. When she reached the desk in the reception room there was no sign of him. She stepped up to the nurse in attendance. "Please - did you see a man pass by here? The one who donated the blood to Midge Jordan? I've got to see him."

"He just left," the nurse informed her. "We tried to persuade him to stay until he got his strength back, but as soon as the doctor told him Miss Jordan would pull through, he left. He drove off a few minutes ago."

Andy stood there dejected. This time Jim had left her without giving her a chance to explain. I guess I deserved that, she thought. How can I ever explain this to him? How can I expect him to believe me? Paul didn't. I only hope Midge does.

She went back to the room where John was waiting. She felt drained. She was elated that Jim was Midge's father and Paul wasn't. Her only regret was that she hadn't known this years ago. John's voice interrupted her thoughts. "I'm going to stay here tonight. I think you should go home and get some rest."

"No, John. Palos Verdes is too far from here. I won't leave until I see Midge. I hope she understands when I tell her that Jim is her real father."

John grinned. "I kinda think she'll be thrilled. She hasn't stopped singing his praises ever since she met him."

"I want to see her as soon as she feels up to talking. The sooner she knows the truth, the better. Do you think you can get me a bed here in the hospital?"

"Let me try," John said. "But promise me you'll get some rest. I can't have two patients on my hands."

Andy nodded. "Please call me as soon as Midge is awake. I should be the one to tell her who donated the blood, and why."

"It's a promise," John said.

Finding a bed didn't take long. Now that Midge was safely out of danger, Andy was able to relax.

She had barely dozed off when she felt herself being nudged. John was standing by her bed.

"Is Midge awake?" she asked.

"She's asking for you," he replied. "It's time to have that talk."

CHAPTER XVIII

Jim sped along the freeway in his Cadillac, headed back toward Santa Barbara.

Finding out that Midge was his daughter changed everything. He was confused. On one hand, he was delighted. He had loved Midge the minute he saw her, and felt the same strong bond she had felt when they first met. Neither one of them had been able to explain it. Now he understood.

But why didn't Andy tell him? Why did she keep it a secret all these years? That's not like Andy, he thought. There has to be some other explanation. But how could she not have known?

He was in a state of shock. He had wanted to stay at the hospital and talk to Midge, but he didn't know what to say.

He drove slowly, weak after giving so much blood. A twenty-four hour coffee shop loomed up ahead, and he decided to stop and get some orange juice and a snack.

He picked up a paper on his way in. It was the evening edition, and there was a report of the accident on the front page, with pictures of Andy and Midge.

"Andy Jordan's daughter in automobile accident," it read. Midge looked so much like Andy. But as he studied the pictures, he saw a striking resemblance to himself. She had his eyes.

A strong sense of love washed over him. I have a daughter! he marveled. I need to talk to her - get to know her better.

Later.

I need time to think.

An hour and a half from the time he left the hospital he drove into his circular driveway. He parked the car in the garage and entered the house and his den.

His emotions were on a roller coaster. He collapsed into his recliner in front of the window that looked out on the ocean. The sound of the waves lulled him to sleep.

He woke with a start. The phone on the end table beside the recliner was ringing.

"Glad you got home safely." John's voice came over the wire, piercing what fogs of sleep remained. "I thought you'd like to know - Midge is awake and doing fine. Andy is in with her now. She doesn't know I'm calling. She wanted to thank you for saving Midge's life, and explain the situation, but you left so abruptly."

Jim was silent. What could he say?

"Jim? Are you still there?" John asked.

Jim cleared his throat. "Yes, I'm here. How is Andy holding up?"

"She's a remarkable woman, Jim," John told him.

Jim took a deep breath. "It's been quite a shock finding out I've had a daughter all these years, and never knew it."

"I can understand that," John agreed. "Jim, Andy didn't know that Midge was your daughter. You have to believe her."

"I want to. You don't know how much I want to. But how could she not know? I thought women knew these things."

"You know, Jim, it's entirely possible for a baby not to be full term. Andy thought Midge was a premie. She told me if she'd had any inkling that you were Midge's father she would have told you. Jim, do you think for one minute she would have had Paul come here all the way from New York knowing he wasn't Midge's father? What was the point? He was the last person she wanted anything to do with."

Jim was silent. What John said made sense, but he was still confused.

"Only an emergency would have impelled Andy to contact him," John continued. "Think about it. Now I think I should join Andy while she explains to Midge that you're her father. She needs my support. I'm sure Midge will be delighted when she finds out. She really loves you. But I should be there with them both. The wedding has been postponed until Midge fully recovers. I'll keep in touch. We can talk later."

He hung up, leaving Jim in a quandary. Should I call Andy? Should I go back to the hospital and confront her?

Not now, he decided. But I've got to find out more about this.

He crawled into bed, and was almost asleep when the phone rang again.

"Hello, Dad." Midge's sweet voice came over the line, loud and clear.

"Midge." He choked back the tears. "My dear daughter," he said when he could bring his voice under control. "How are you feeling?"

"Just fine, thanks to you. I know this is going to sound strange, but in a way I'm glad this accident happened. If it hadn't, we might never have known that you're my Dad. I want you to know that I'm more than happy about this. I'm ecstatic! I've been wishing you were my father, and to find out it's actually true is like - it's like - I've gone to heaven. Somehow I'm not surprised that Paul isn't my father. I never felt any kinship with him. But you - I felt it the minute I met you. Oh, Jim - I mean - Dad - I couldn't be happier! It's the best wedding present I could ever receive!"

Tears rolled down Jim's face at her words. He reached for his hankie and quickly wiped them away. "Midge, I want to come and see you, but I don't know how your mother feels about all this."

"Honestly, Dad, she never had the slightest inkling. But I know she's as happy about this as I am. She's been miserable with Dad - I mean - Paul."

"I know she has," Jim agreed.

"Maybe this will bring you two together," Midge suggested.

Jim was silent for a moment. "I don't know, Midge. So much has happened that needs to be resolved."

"Well - you're still going to walk me down the aisle, aren't you? I'll be terribly disappointed if you don't."

"Of course, Midge. I wouldn't miss it. Especially now. Does your mother know that you asked me?"

"No. I'm waiting for the right time to tell her."

"Have you set another date for the wedding?"

"Not yet. We're going to wait until I've fully recovered. I'm leaving the hospital day after tomorrow and going to Mom's house. My ribs will be healed soon. Dad - "

"Yes, dear - what is it?"

"I want to meet you somewhere alone. We need to talk and get acquainted - really acquainted. As soon as I feel strong enough I want to drive up to Santa Barbara to see you. Please say I can come."

Jim was delighted. "Any time you can make it I'll be here waiting. Just let me know. Maybe you can plan to stay for a real visit."

"I'll see what I can do," Midge promised. "I'll call and let you know when to expect me." Her voice broke. "Dad - I love you."

She hung up, leaving Jim dissolved in tears. His life had been so empty, and now it was suddenly full. The woman he loved most in the whole world next to Andy he had just found out was his very own daughter.

CHAPTER XVIX

Midge had been at Andy's home in Palos Verdes for a month recuperating. She kept in touch with Jim on a regular basis. She wanted to invite him to come to Palos Verdes, but hesitated, not knowing how Andy would feel about it. It might put her in an awkward position.

Neither the trauma of the accident, nor having to postpone the wedding, interfered one iota with her joy at finding out that Jim was her real father. She couldn't wait until she felt well enough to drive to Santa Barbara. Her ribs were almost completely healed. The soreness was gone, and her strength had returned.

One morning she woke up and felt the time had come. It was seven o'clock. She showered and dressed in her jeans and plaid shirt. After putting on her running shoes with the velcro straps, she walked into the kitchen where Andy was fixing breakfast. She put her head back and sniffed. "Mm! Something smells awfully good. What are you cooking?"

"Midge!" Andy greeted her. "How are you feeling, dear?"

Midge stretched. "Great! As good as new! I think I'll sign up for the 10K run!" she said, joking.

Andy looked concerned. "Don't push it, dear. Take it one day at a time."

Midge grimaced. "That's what I've been doing, and I'm getting bored."

Andy gave her a motherly smile. "I was just about to bring you some pancakes and bacon." She put the food on two plates and brought them over to the table in front of the window that faced the ocean.

The view was spectacular this morning. The incredible blue of the ocean, and the white crests of the waves, defied the imagination. The scenery was an artist's dream. The trees were blowing slightly in the wind that had just come up, and the seagulls and pelicans soared and banked in perfect formation. A tiny sparrow landed on the window sill and looked in, proudly preening its feathers.

"Dive in!" Andy ordered. "I don't make pancakes every day, so take advantage."

Midge ate heartily. "This sure beats hospital food," she remarked. She put her fork down and looked at Andy. "Mom, I need to get away for a few days. I'm tired of being an invalid." She stared out the window for a moment, not knowing how her mother would react. "Mom, I want to go and see Dad."

"What!" Andy exclaimed. "After all he's done? I think it's a bad idea with the divorce coming up. I haven't heard from him since he went back to New York. He was very angry - "

Midge interrupted. "Mom - I said Dad, not Paul."

"Oh!" Andy looked relieved. "But - dear - do you think you feel up to that long drive?"

"I'm fine," she assured Andy. "I told Dad I'd be up to see him as soon as I felt well enough, and I want to go. Today. I plan to stay for a few days. Dad and I have a lot of catching up to do."

"Yes, I know," Andy agreed. "You two need time alone. I just want you to be sure you're ready."

Midge smiled tenderly at her mother. "Mom, you and Dad have given me the best wedding present you could possibly give me." Her eyes filled with tears. "I have a real Dad now, and I want to get to know him." She rose from her chair. "Is there anything you want me to tell him?"

Andy averted her eyes. "No, dear. I don't think he'd be interested in anything I have to say."

"I don't believe that for one minute!" Midge exclaimed. "Mom, he loves you. He always has. I'm hoping and praying that you two get together again. He's the one you should have married in the first place. I want us to put all those unhappy years with Paul behind us and start over."

Andy looked wistful. "That would be wonderful, but I think it's a little late. I treated Jim badly, and I shouldn't expect him to give me another chance."

"But you'd like it, wouldn't you?" Midge asked, pressing her for an answer.

Andy had a faraway look in her eyes. "In a heartbeat," she sighed. "But the most important thing is for you and Jim to get to know each other. Too much time has gone by already. As long as you feel up to it, go! With my blessing. Give Jim my best. I don't think he believes that I didn't know he was your father."

"Well, I believe you!" Midge declared. "I know you love me too much to have subjected me to all those miserable years with Paul unless you really thought he was my father. Boy, am I glad he isn't!"

Andy smiled. "So am I, dear. I'm just as glad as you are. I really blew it when I married Paul. Looking back on it, I wonder how I could have been so stupid." She changed the subject. "Maddi called me last night. They want me to come back to New York. As long as you won't be needing me here, I'll see if they have space on the eleven o'clock plane this morning. You can use my car to drive to Santa Barbara. I won't be needing it."

"Thanks, Mom." Midge went over to the phone and dialed Santa Barbara. Jim answered on the second ring.

"Dad, I'm driving up today to see you. Is that okay?"

"I had a feeling you'd call," Jim answered. "Are you sure you feel strong enough?"

Midge laughed. "You couldn't stop me! I'll be leaving as soon as I pack a few things. I plan to stay for a few days. Expect me in a couple of hours. I love you, Dad." She hung up.

"You stay with Jim as long as you want," Andy said. "I know you'll be in good hands. Maybe after a few days John could join you."

"I doubt it," Midge replied. "He has a busy schedule. Don't worry about me, Mom."

"What about the wedding? Have you and John made any further plans?"

"Not yet. But we will soon. I'll let you know. I have to pack."

In fifteen minutes she returned with her suitcase. "Have a good flight to New York, Mom. I'll tell Dad you've been called back there, and I can stay as long as he wants me to." She hugged her mother and left.

The drive to Santa Barbara was relaxing and leisurely, in spite of the remaining trauma from what she had been through. She took her time and drove carefully. "One accident is plenty," she murmured under her breath. She shook off the memory and allowed the beauty of the day to take over.

Somehow I have to find a way to erase any doubt Dad has about Mom, she thought as she drove along. They've been given what many people never get - a second chance. They can't blow it! They just can't!

It was a beautiful autumn day, and as Midge drank in the scenery, she could see a few liquid amber trees that hadn't yet shed their leaves. The brilliant magenta colored leaves were spectacular. The top was down on her mother's Jaguar convertible, and Midge's long, blond hair blew freely. Just knowing she would soon be with her real Dad lifted her spirits, and she knew nothing could go wrong.

In slightly over an hour and a half from the time she left Andy's home she drove into the driveway in Santa Barbara.

Jim was outside watching for her.

She jumped out of the car and ran to meet him.

They rushed into each other's arms. After a few minutes of laughing and crying they went into the house.

Jim had fixed a delicious lunch - a fresh chicken salad with pineapple chunks, and sliced pecans. They took their plates outside by the ocean. The birds were singing and the waves were crashing into the rocks below. The sweet scent of perfume from the jasmine bushes wafted over to them as they ate. It was so peaceful, it seemed that there couldn't be anything but peace everywhere. There was no room for anything else.

Midge was the happiest she had ever been, except for the time when John proposed to her. She looked up to see Jim smiling at her.

"Andy told me you love to play golf," he said. "I can set up a game at my club if you like. Or we can do it some other time if you'd rather."

"Don't feel you have to entertain me, Dad. I'm here because I want us to get acquainted. If you don't mind, I'd just as soon do it some other time. It's so beautiful here, I'd like to just sit and enjoy it with you."

Jim reached out and took her hand. "I was hoping you'd say that. There's plenty of time for golf."

He gazed at the ocean. The air seemed laden with unanswered questions.

Midge sensed that he wanted to say something, but felt a little hesitant about it. "What, Dad?" she asked.

"How's your mother?"

"Mom's fine. She took the eleven o'clock plane back to New York. She got a call last night, and she's needed there. She'll be staying at the same hotel."

"Has she heard from Paul?"

"Not a word."

"Do you think she'll be seeing him in New York?"

Midge snorted. "Hardly! The last she heard from him, he left in a huff before you arrived for the transfusion. As usual, he didn't wait to see if I was going to be all right. He accused Mom of knowing all along that he wasn't my father, and said he was going to use that to get a huge settlement in the divorce."

Jim shook his head. "Why doesn't that surprise me?" he said. "It sounds just like him. Do you think he'll be able to?"

"I hope not." Midge was silent for a moment. "Dad - Mom had no idea that Paul wasn't my father. She would never have allowed him to treat me the way he did if she had known. She would have left him long ago and taken me with her. Why would she have dragged him all the way from New York for my transfusion, knowing he wasn't my father? It makes no sense. I wish you'd believe her."

Jim nodded. "It was a shock when I first found out you were my daughter, I didn't know what to believe. I was confused. But I've been giving it a lot of thought since then, and there's too much that doesn't add up. It isn't like Andy. I know she would have told me if she had known. I wish I could tell her that, but I doubt if she wants anything to do with me now. I should never have doubted her, and I'm not sure she can forgive me for that."

"You're wrong, Dad. She loves you, and love can forgive anything. She feels that you can never forgive her for jilting you years ago. That puts you two at sort of an impasse, doesn't it? One of you will have to make the first move."

Jim nodded. "But which one? That's the question."

Midge decided to be direct. "Do you still love Mom?"

Jim was just as direct. "I never stopped loving her."

Midge grew pensive. Suddenly she turned to Jim. "Dad, I've got a dandy idea!" Her eyes danced with delight just thinking about it.

Jim smiled at her tenderly. "You look just like your mother. When we were engaged years ago, that's how she looked when she was cooking up some scheme. What is it?"

"First, Mom's divorce will have to be final. I hope it's before Christmas." She leaned over and kissed him. "This is going to work - I know it will! Won't Mom be surprised!"

"Hey, how about letting me in on this?"

"I'll tell you as soon as I get all the details straight in my mind," Midge told him. "Trust me!"

CHAPTER XX

As soon as Midge drove off for Santa Barbara, Andy called Richard. She was all packed and ready to leave for the airport. Richard said he would pick her up in ten minutes and drive her, and they would discuss the progress of the divorce on the way.

She had just sent a Fax to Maddi telling her when to expect her when she heard the doorbell. That must be Richard. He's early.

She opened the door, but it wasn't Richard. A messenger handed her an envelope and left just as Richard drove up. The envelope had the return address of a lawyer in New York.

Richard hopped out of the car and hurried up to the door. "What is it, Andy? That's not from Paul, is it?"

"I have a funny feeling it is." She handed the unopened envelope to him.

Richard entered the house and sat down. He opened the envelope and pulled out a document. A deep frown creased his forehead as he read it. He put the document on his lap and looked at her. "I'm shocked," he said. "And yet - I'm not all that surprised. It's just what I'd expect from that bastard!" He got up and began to pace, still looking at the document.

Andy was frightened. "What is it, Richard?"

Richard handed her the paper. "It's from Paul's lawyer. Paul is accusing you of infidelity. He claims you deliberately deceived him into thinking he was Midge's father. He's demanding that you sell the house and turn the entire assets over to him, and he wants half of everything you make from your writing."

Andy's knees started to give way, and Richard caught her just in time. He sat her down on the sofa until she could regain her sense of balance. "Oh, Richard, he can't do that, can he? That's not fair!"

Richard looked at her long and hard. "Andy, I think you'd better tell me everything, so I'll know how to fight this in court." He picked up her suitcase and opened the front door. "Tell me on the way to the airport, or you'll miss your plane." Andy set the alarm and locked the door. After all that Paul had put her through, it was too much for her to think he might get away with this. By the time they reached the airport she had explained everything to Richard.

"Is that all?" he asked. "You didn't leave anything out?"

"That's it," Andy told him. "He's accusing me of being unfaithful to him but this all happened before I met Paul, and it only happened once. I've never been unfaithful to Paul."

Richard snorted. "He's the one who's been unfaithful. If it becomes necessary, I'll testify to that."

"Richard, I honestly thought Paul was Midge's father. I had no idea - not even an inkling - that he wasn't. What am I going to do? I inherited the house from my parents. How can he demand that I sell it and give him the money? And what about our joint account? He closed it out and never told me. I learned about it from the bank. How can he sue me for everything?" Her voice trembled.

"We'll handle this," Richard assured her. "He won't get one red cent if I have anything to say about it."

Traffic was heavy, and when they arrived at the airport the cars were all lined up - two abreast. Richard was able to stop just long enough to let Andy out and deposit her suitcase on the trolley, ready for it to be checked through.

"Stop worrying," he said as he got back into the car. "We can fight this. Have a good flight. I'll talk to you later."

He drove off, leaving Andy worried and sick at heart.

She entered the building and picked up her ticket. Will I ever be rid of Paul and his schemes? she lamented. How I wish Jim were here! He'd know what to do.

Then a sudden thought hit her. What if Paul tries to drag Jim into this? I should warn him! She pondered this all the way to New York, and was so upset she couldn't touch the food the flight attendant brought to her.

It was almost seven o'clock in the evening New York time when the plane landed, and Maddi was waiting with the limousine.

"Hi!" she greeted Andy. "Am I glad to see you! We've been trying to handle things here by ourselves, but we really need you. How is Midge?"

Andy managed a faint smile. "Midge is fine. She's with - uh - " She had been about to say she's with her father, but Maddi knew nothing about this. If the media should get hold of it they would have a heyday! Could this hurt the sale of the book? Oh, my God! I have to tell her and Sonny so they'll be prepared! Her face paled. This sudden revelation combined with her empty stomach caused her to feel weak, and she stumbled.

Maddi grabbed her arm. "Are you all right?" she asked.

By this time they had reached the limousine and Maddi rushed her into it. As soon as they were seated and had pulled away from the curb, Maddi repeated her question.

"Maddi, there's something I have to tell you," Andy said. "You may want to wash your hands of me when I do. It might cause a scandal."

"I'm listening. I'm sure it's not that bad."

"I don't really know where to start," Andy told her. "It goes way back to two weeks before I met Paul." She swallowed, then proceeded to tell her the whole story.

When she finished, Maddi burst out laughing. This was the last thing Andy expected.

Maddi finally stopped laughing and wiped her eyes. "Sounds like your next novel," she chuckled. "What great publicity! The public will love it! It shows you're human. Everyone will rush to buy the book!"

"They will?"

"Andy, if the media gets hold of it, it will help, not hinder!"

The limousine pulled up to the entrance of the hotel. Andy got out and the bellman came out to pick up her luggage.

As she started to leave, Maddi lowered the car window and stuck her head out. "Are you hungry?" she asked. "Maybe you'd like to grab a bite with Sonny and me. The bellman can take your luggage up to your room. You're already checked in. I took care of it before I came to the airport."

Andy wasn't looking forward to eating alone. She hopped back into the limousine. "Where to?" she asked.

"How about that new restaurant in Central Park - the Canterbury Tails? Lobster tails are their specialty. Sound good?" Without waiting for an answer Maddi picked up the car phone. "I'll call Sonny and tell him to meet us there."

It didn't take long to reach Central Park. They drove up the long driveway under the archway of maple trees crowned with deep autumn hues. The shaded walkway provided shelter from the slight breeze that was blowing.

They entered the building and walked through the gift shop filled with all kinds of intriguing relics, which would ordinarily have captured Andy's interest. But she was too bogged down by Paul's threats to pay much attention.

As they walked up to the desk, the maitre d' greeted Maddi by name. One of the hostesses ushered them upstairs to the dimly lit cocktail lounge where they decided to wait for Sonny.

"I think you could use a drink," Maddi told Andy. "What's your favorite?"

"I'm not much of a drinker," Andy confessed. "Maybe just a white wine. I haven't eaten since breakfast. I don't want to weave out of here. That would be one for the publicity hounds!"

She reached for the peanuts that were in a bowl on the table.

Maddi motioned to the waiter. She ordered the wine for Andy and a Martini for herself.

As Andy sipped her wine she relaxed. It was so peaceful here. As she looked out the window, she could see the lake and people walking and riding bicycles. Across from the lounge was a dance floor where an orchestra was rehearsing. Music with the big band sound wafted across the aisle and into the cocktail lounge. As Andy sipped her wine the feeling of impending doom began to lift. They had been there only a few minutes when Sonny arrived. They picked up their drinks and headed downstairs and out to the ivy covered patio.

It was sunset by now, and the strings of tiny lights that wound around the tree trunks twinkled gaily as dusk set in. The September air was just starting to show signs of cooling, and an electric heater hovered over the table to keep them warm.

Andy was still apprehensive about Paul's threats, but at least her worries about a scandal had been put to rest.

"We've missed you, Andy," Sonny told her as soon as they ordered. "How's Midge doing?"

"Just fine," Andy replied. "Otherwise I wouldn't be here."

"They've been clamoring for you at the bookstores," he told her. "It's not the same without the author there to sign her autograph."

Andy looked around and smiled. "I've missed all this. I didn't think I would, but I guess it kind of grew on me. I really love New York." She laughed. "I never thought I'd say that."

"How's the divorce coming?" Sonny asked her.

Andy shrugged. "Paul is giving me a hard time."

"Oh. Sorry to hear that. Is there anything we can do?"

"Thanks, Sonny, but I don't think so. Richard, my lawyer, is doing everything that can be done at this stage."

"Has Midge set another date for the wedding?" Maddi asked her.

"Not yet." Andy looked at Sonny, then back at Maddi. "I think Sonny should know what's going on, don't you?"

Maddi proceeded to tell him what Andy had told her.

Sonny had the same reaction as Maddi. "What great publicity!" he exclaimed. "People will think you're a real femme fatale!"

Andy blushed. "I don't know whether I like that or not."

"You'll like the boost it'll give to the sales!" Sonny promised her.

"I just hope Paul doesn't get his hands on any of my royalties." Andy sounded pessimistic.

Sonny leaned back in his chair and smiled. "I have an answer to that. We can set up a trust fund under Midge's name just for your royalties, with you as Trustee. No one will be able to touch it except you and Midge. You'll have a code you can punch in any time you need some money, and Paul won't be able to get his hands on it."

Andy felt her body begin to relax. "Thank you, Sonny! I think that calls for a toast!"

Sonny motioned to the waitress, and ordered another round. By this time their food had come, and Andy felt another knot in her stomach untie itself. She was famished. It was almost eight-thirty at night, New York time - ten and a half hours without food.

As soon as they finished eating, Andy rose from her chair and threw her coat around her shoulders. "I'm a little tired," she said. "I'd better get back to the hotel and get some rest. What are the plans for tomorrow?"

"We've booked you for another session at the Star Bookstore at ten o'clock. We'll pick you up at nine. We reported it to the newspapers, so we expect a big crowd."

"I'll be ready," Andy promised.

The limousine was waiting by the front door. As they exited, Andy was suddenly surrounded by fans wanting her autograph.

She was stunned. How did they know she was at this restaurant? The tension returned.

Word gets around, she thought, and she wondered when word of her divorce and Paul's suit would hit the papers.

They soon arrived at the hotel.

After picking up her key, Andy went up to her room. She was exhausted - not only from the flight, but her emotional state was far from peaceful. She decided to go directly to bed and get a good night's sleep, ready for the onslaught tomorrow.

CHAPTER XXI

Paul was fixing a TV dinner in his lush new condo. How he hated eating in! The food was terrible, but he didn't have the money to dine out in the lavish style he felt he deserved.

He looked around at the elegant furnishings. At least I'm out of that awful hell hole I was in! I suppose I should be grateful. But it's not enough. I should be able to live in the style I like.

As he ate, he picked up the paper. A picture of Andy taken yesterday as she came out of the Canterbury Tails restaurant stared up at him. She's really living it up, he mused. Expensive restaurants, expensive hotels, expensive shows.

Never mind, he promised himself. I'll get my credit card back if it's the last thing I do!

He was halfway through his dinner when the doorbell rang. A messenger handed him a manila envelope.

It was from Richard.

Andy was countersuing him for her half of the five hundred thousand dollars he had withdrawn from their joint account.

Paul smirked. "They'll never find it!" he vowed.

There was a letter enclosed from Richard to him personally. As he read it, his inflated, cocky ego flattened out like a pancake. The letter stated that because he had deserted Andy to play around with other women, and taken her half of the money from their joint account, there was no way he could win a settlement.

It also stated that if he persisted in this suit that he, Richard, would be forced to disclose the fact that Paul had once tried to molest Midge.

Paul picked up the phone and dialed his lawyer. "Stan," he said, "I just got a document and a letter from Andy's lawyer. He said that - "

"I know what it says," Stan interrupted. "I have a copy. Did you have an affair with her lawyer's wife? Did you walk out on your wife so you could date other women? Did you close out your joint account and leave nothing for her to live on? Did you hide the money and expect her to pay all your extravagant bills? Did you try to molest Midge?"

Paul was so overwhelmed by blow after blow of these accusations that for a moment he was speechless.

"Never mind," the lawyer told him. "Your silence speaks for itself. You weren't honest with me, Paul. I need complete honesty. I can't handle your case. All this would have come up at the divorce hearing, and I'd be left hanging, not knowing how to defend you. We'd be laughed out of court. I'll send you a bill for what you owe me."

There was a dial tone as the lawyer hung up. Paul slammed the phone down and picked up the dinner he hadn't finished. He hurled it across the room. It flew through the open glass doors and landed on the floor of the terrace.

He grabbed his jacket and left. After walking several blocks, he found himself at the edge of Central Park, where he sat down on a bench to think.

I've got to get my hands on some money. I can't touch Andy's private account until she's dead. There has to be another way.

He sat there for half an hour - thinking - scheming. Then, with an exclamation of triumph, he knew exactly what to do. He rose from the bench and returned to his condo.

As soon as he got there he picked up the phone and dialed Andy.

Her line was busy.

He tried again.

Still busy.

He slammed the phone down impatiently. Now that he had made up his mind what had to be done, he couldn't wait to carry it out. Finally the phone was free, and Andy answered on the first ring. "Maddi?" she asked. "Have plans been changed?"

"This isn't Maddi," Paul informed her. "I have a proposition. Where can I meet you?"

Andy emitted an exasperated sigh. "Paul, how many times do I have to tell you - anything you have to say you can say to Richard. He's handling everything."

"I don't think you'd want him to handle this," Paul told her. "This is strictly between you and me. Where can I meet you?"

"I'm not meeting you anywhere," Andy told him. "What do you want? Can't you tell me on the phone?"

"No, Andy. Someone might be listening in."

"Look, Paul - I was just about to go to bed. I have a hectic day coming up."

"This has to be said in person," Paul persisted. "You want the divorce, don't you? If you don't want your name dragged through the mud, you'd better hear me out."

"Paul, I'm not going out again tonight. If you insist on seeing me, I'll meet you in the cocktail lounge here at the hotel. But this had better be important."

"I'll be there in twenty minutes," Paul said.

When Paul arrived, Andy was already there, dressed in jeans and a sweater. The place was empty.

"Okay," Andy said. "What's this all about, Paul?"

"Can I buy you a drink?" he asked her.

"No, thanks. Just tell me what's on your mind so I can go back to my room."

Several people had entered the bar by this time, and Paul looked around, fidgeting. "You know," he said, "on second thought, I think this might be better said in the privacy of your room."

Andy started to protest.

"This will only take a few minutes," Paul interrupted. "Once we come to an agreement, I'll be on my way. I think you'll find it worth your while. You don't want a scene here, do you?"

Andy stood up and Paul followed her to the elevator.

As soon as they were in her room, Andy turned and faced him. "Okay," she said. "Let's get this over with. What do you want?"

Paul looked triumphant. "I don't know if you've thought about this, but I'm sure you wouldn't want it spread all over the newspapers that you were unfaithful to me, and gave birth to a child fathered by another man."

"Is that it?" Andy asked him.

"All I want is enough money to live the kind of life I like. You'll be making plenty with your book, and any future books you may write. I understand some authors make millions a year. How about it, Andy? Give me a generous allowance each month, or I'll go to the papers with my story."

For a moment Andy said nothing. Then she chuckled. "That's blackmail, Paul. It's a crime."

Paul shrugged. "So report me. But remember, if you do, the scandal will hit the papers. The media will eat it up. I could even sell my story to the tabloids. Either way, I win. Take your choice. I'm sure you wouldn't want me to go to your publisher with this juicy bit of gossip."

Andy burst out laughing as she opened the door. "Please leave, Paul. Maddi and Sonny already know the whole story, and they're not afraid of the scandal. They say it would only sell more books."

This left Paul momentarily speechless. She had called his bluff, and shown that she wasn't afraid of exposure.

"Go, Paul!" Andy ordered. "I've had enough of your shananigans. Go right now, or I'll call security."

"I'll call the papers!" he threatened.

"Go ahead. Do anything you want. Just get out of my sight."

Paul left and went back to his condo to rethink his strategy. He had been sure Andy would pay him money to keep the story out of the papers. Now he realized he'd been stupid, and had only succeeded in giving her and Richard more ammunition to use against him.

He had to do something to keep her from exposing him as a blackmailer. And he had to find a way to get his hands on her private account and her royalties. He knew it had to be done before the divorce became final. Otherwise, he would forfeit community property and inherit nothing. If what Richard had said was true, he couldn't count on getting any kind of a settlement in the divorce.

As he pondered this, he realized there was only one solution. He didn't like it, but it was the only way.

She's given me no other choice. I'll do whatever it takes, he decided. *I've got to get my hands on that money!*

CHAPTER XXII

As soon as Paul left, Andy called Richard in Los Angeles and told him what Paul had proposed.

Richard was jubilant. "Andy, Paul is hanging himself! This is blackmail! It's one more thing we can use against him at the divorce hearing! I bet he's scared stiff we'll report him. Watch your step. There's no telling what he may think of next. He's getting desperate. His lawyer called and told me he quit the case, so Paul is without a lawyer now."

"Oh, I can't believe he'd harm me, if that's what you're thinking. I'm not surprised at the blackmail, but harm me? I don't think so. But I'll be careful."

"Perhaps you should hire a bodyguard," Richard suggested.

Andy laughed. "I have plenty of bodyguards, with Maddi and Sonny. They're always protecting me," she assured him. "Do you know yet where Paul hid the money?"

"We're working on it. It could be in Switzerland, or the Cayman Islands - or even somewhere in Canada. We'll find it."

Andy felt a lot more confident now about the outcome of the divorce. She didn't see how Paul could get half of her royalties, or the entire proceeds from the sale of the house. And even if Richard couldn't find the money that Paul hid, her own private account was rebuilding itself substantially with interest now that Paul no longer had a credit card. And the new trust fund she had opened with the royalties from her book was growing. She was already working on her next novel, and was well able to take care of herself. She hopped into bed and slept soundly.

Early the next morning she was up and ready for the day's signing. When they arrived at the bookstore the line of people covered two blocks. Andy couldn't believe it! To think that only a few months ago she was leading a humdrum life, and now - well, to say the least, life was very exciting.

Everything had fallen into place - - almost everything. Her book was a huge success, and Midge, her beloved daughter, was getting married, and finally had the father she deserved to have.

But in spite of all that, Andy felt a deep void in her own life. She missed Jim terribly. If it was possible she loved him more each day. Her eyes filled with tears just thinking about him.

She shook it off. He's washed his hands of me. Get used to it!

The line of customers grew longer as the day wore on, and the owner of the bookstore was finally forced to set up a sign that said they were closing in five minutes.

Andy was relieved. It had been a long, hard day, and she was looking forward to the quiet, relaxing dinner that Maddi and Sonny had planned for her. They decided to eat at the hotel, so she could retire immediately afterwards.

Her phone was ringing as she entered her room, and she hurried over to it.

Paul again!

Andy had just about had it with him. "Paul, I told you - anything you have to say, tell it to Richard."

"Andy, I just called to apologize. I've put you through hell. Can you ever find it in your heart to forgive me?"

Andy was stunned. Was this sincere or just another ploy?

"Perhaps we should have a farewell drink," Paul continued. "I could meet you in the cocktail lounge at your hotel. What do you say? Just to show there are no hard feelings."

Before Andy could think of an answer, Paul offered her the perfect enticement.

"I'll tell you where I put the joint account," he promised.

Andy knew he was baiting her, but figured it would be worth it to find out where he hid the money. Perhaps just this once won't hurt, she figured. The divorce will be final soon and he'll be out of my life for good. "Okay," she agreed. "But I can't stay. I have a busy day ahead."

"This won't take long," he told her. "See you in fifteen minutes."

He arrived right on time.

Strange, Andy thought. He was always late for everything.

Has he changed, or is he trying to impress me? What is he up to? Stop being paranoid, she chided herself.

Paul led her to a table in a secluded corner. "How about a couple of Margaritas?"

"Whatever you think," Andy told him.

Paul motioned to the waiter. "Two Margaritas, please."

As he pulled out his wallet to pay the waiter a small empty plastic bag fell out of his pocket.

Andy noticed that it had pink and blue colored stripes along the zipper. Must be one of those new sandwich bags, she figured. Is he so strapped for money that he has to "brown bag" it?

"What's that for?" she asked.

Paul appeared flustered. He stuffed his wallet and the plastic bag back into his pocket. "Oh, n-nothing," he stammered. "Uh - do you mind if we put this on your tab? I'll pay you back."

"That's not necessary, Paul," she quickly assured him.

"It's okay," he replied. "I'm coming into some money very soon - uh - from a distant relative."

What distant relative? Andy wondered. He doesn't have any relatives that I know of. She gave the waiter her room number. "Put this on my tab, please."

She gave Paul a penetrating stare, then came right to the point. "Where's the money, Paul?"

"It's tucked away safely in a bank on the Cayman Islands under both our names. I only took it because I knew it would make a lot more money on the interest there. I did it for you."

Andy was skeptical. "Why are you so short of cash? Surely you can use some of that money to - "

"I can't touch it," he interrupted. "They require a minimum balance of at least five hundred thousand dollars. I've been living on the interest. It's not nearly enough. Everything is so expensive these days."

"Especially if you spend money like water," she mumbled under her breath.

Paul ignored her remark. But as she sipped her drink, he suddenly exclaimed - "Oh, look!" and pointed toward the lobby. "Isn't that one of your publishers looking for you?"

Andy rose from the table and went out into the lobby, but she didn't see either Maddi or Sonny. "Was there anyone here looking for me?" she asked the clerk at the desk.

"No, Mrs. Jordan."

"Oh," she said, puzzled. "Thank you."

"Were they your publishers?" Paul asked her as she returned to the lounge.

"No, it wasn't them."

"Oh. Sorry," Paul said. "I could have sworn - oh, well, it doesn't matter." He held his glass up. "Here's to an amicable divorce," he toasted.

Andy picked up her glass and took a sip of her drink. It tasted a little dryer than before - almost bitter. After several more sips she felt a little strange. "I think I'd better get up to my room," she told Paul. "I'm very tired, and I need some rest." Her speech was a little slurred.

"Of course," he agreed.

She left her unfinished drink on the table. As she exited the lounge, she looked back just in time to see Paul pour the remainder of her Margarita into the plastic bag. What a weird thing to do! she thought. Is he doggie-bagging it to drink later?

Half way to the elevator she stumbled and sat down in a chair in the lobby in an effort to steady herself. As she sat there she saw Paul walk to the men's restroom with the plastic bag in his hand. He was carrying it very carefully. At this point she was too groggy to try and figure it out.

She rose from the chair and groped her way to the elevator.

She entered her room and staggered across the floor. What's the matter with me? she thought in a panic. I've never felt like this. She slipped her clothes off and managed to don her nightie before falling to the floor. The room began to spin. She grabbed hold of the bed sheets and sat up, trying to regain her equilibrium.

"Something's wrong!" she cried out in a panic. A mental picture of Paul pouring her drink into the plastic bag flashed across her mind.

Then she remembered what Richard had said.

"Be careful. You don't know what Paul might think of next. He's a desperate man."

Did he just try to kill me? No! No! I can't believe that!

She reached out for the phone on the night stand.

She managed to press the button marked "Operator."

"Help!" she whispered into the phone, and lost consciousness.

CHAPTER XXIII

"She's still unconscious," Andy heard someone say.

She tried to snap out of it, but couldn't.

Then she heard Sonny's voice. It sounded hollow and far away. "Andy - Andy, can you hear me?" he kept asking.

"How long has she been like this?" she heard Maddi ask.

"About two hours," a strange voice replied. "I've been her doctor since they brought her in. Who is she? What happened?"

"Andy Jordan, the writer," Sonny answered. "We're her publishers. I got a call from the clerk at the hotel. He told me the ambulance had taken her to the hospital."

Andy tried to speak, but couldn't make a sound.

"She was poisoned," she heard the doctor say. "I recognized the signs when they brought her in. Either someone poisoned her or she tried to commit suicide. She must have felt faint and passed out. We pumped her stomach. Thank God she didn't imbibe much of the poison and they got her here in time."

Then she heard Maddi's anxious voice. "She's going to recover, isn't she?"

"We're doing everything we can," the doctor told her.

"How long will it take?"

"It's hard to say."

Andy tried to move her lips, but they felt as though they weighed a ton. Her throat hurt so much she could barely swallow. She heard a moan and realized it was her own voice trying to speak.

"Andy - Andy, can you hear me?" It was Sonny's voice again. He held her hand. "Andy, if you can hear me, please squeeze my hand. Please, Andy - try!"

Andy managed to make her fingers move. In a daze she heard Maddi's voice. "I think she's trying to come out of it!"

The next thing Andy was aware of was a blur of faces. She blinked and gradually the faces became clear. A strange man hovered over her.

Must be the doctor, she figured, and she realized she was in a hospital. "Maddi - Sonny," she whispered. "I'm glad you're here."

"Andy, what happened?" they asked.

Slowly the fuzz of memory cleared, and she remembered her meeting with Paul, and his telling her that Maddi and Sonny were in the lobby.

Could he have diverted her attention so he could put something into her drink? It was the only logical explanation. The doctor said she had been poisoned. How could he do this to her? But she knew why. "Paul - Paul - " she muttered.

"What about Paul?" Sonny demanded. "Did he do this to you?"

Andy spoke so low that they had to lean down to hear her. "I think so," she mumbled.

As she drifted off she heard the doctor say, "She's asleep. She'll be okay now. She needs her rest. Please come back later."

But Andy's sleep was far from restful. She never thought Paul would stoop to murder, but she knew without a doubt that he was guilty.

When she woke up an hour later, Maddi and Sonny were standing by her bed. She smiled, grateful to be alive. "What time is it?" she asked.

"Eleven o'clock in the evening," Maddi told her.

Sonny spoke to her gently but firmly. "Andy, please tell us what happened. How did Paul do this? I thought you were avoiding him."

"I was." Andy grimaced. "He wanted us to have a drink together to show there were no hard feelings. A farewell drink, he said. Some farewell! Where's the phone? I have to call my lawyer."

"I think you should talk to the police first," Sonny advised her. "I suspected foul play and I called them. The detective is waiting outside. I'll get him."

The detective entered Andy's room with a notebook and pen in hand. "Tell me what happened," he said. "Don't leave out anything."

Andy told him every detail she could remember.

The detective nodded and closed the notebook. "I'm going over to the Park Plaza and question the bartender. Maybe he noticed something. You say that Paul took the plastic bag to the men's restroom? I'll check the waste receptacle. It should be easy to spot with the pink and blue zipper."

"I'll go with you," Sonny offered. "Maybe I can help."

"I'd better go alone," the detective told him. "I'm going to assign a bodyguard outside this door, but until he gets here, I want you two to stay with Mrs. Jordan. She needs protection." He looked grim as he spoke to Andy. "I strongly advise you to make sure the press hears nothing about this until I've had a chance to look into it. If your husband has any inkling that you're recovering, he might try this again. I'll keep you posted."

As the detective left, the doctor entered the room and smiled at Andy. "You're feeling better, I see."

"Doctor, please get me a phone," she said. "I have to speak to my lawyer. He should know what happened." She tried to sit up.

Maddi rushed over and pressed the button to raise the bed. "What's his number?" she asked.

Andy gave her his home number. Maddi dialed it and handed the phone to Andy.

It was a little after eight in the evening in California with the time difference. "Who is this?" Richard asked.

"It's Andy."

"Andy? You sound so hoarse. Are you all right?"

"I am now," Andy replied. "Paul just tried to kill me."

"What?!"

"I'm in the hospital. They got me here in time, but they had to pump my stomach. That's why I sound hoarse."

Richard was appalled. "How did this happen?"

"Paul wanted to meet for a farewell drink," she explained.

"Why?!"

"He wanted us to say goodbye as friends. Some friendship!"

"Are you sure Paul did this?"

"He's the only one who could have." She went on to explain what happened.

"My God!" Richard exclaimed. "How could he do that to you?!"

"Richard, he knows he can't get any of my royalties or what's in my private bank account, or any proceeds from the sale of the house as long as I'm alive. You told me he was desperate, but I never suspected he'd go this far."

"Are you sure you're all right?"

"I'm fine. Maddi and Sonny are here, and the doctor has taken excellent care of me. Sonny called the police. The detective wants me to stay in the hospital for a few days."

"So Paul won't know you're recovering!" Richard interrupted. "Good thinking!"

"Richard, would you please call Midge and tell her I'm all right? If she's not at her home she'll be in Santa Barbara with Jim. I'll give you both numbers. Please tell her not to worry. It would be awful if the reporters got hold of this and she heard it on the news first. Tell her to steer clear of reporters. They might try to pump her for information."

"I'll call her right away," he promised. "I'm surprised you agreed to meet with Paul," he chided her. "What were you thinking?"

"I wasn't going to, but when he said he'd tell me where he hid the money - - "

"He tricked you, Andy," Richard interrupted. "Did he tell you where it is?"

"He said it's in a bank in the Cayman Islands. It gets a higher rate of interest there. He said it's under both our names."

"I doubt that!" Richard snorted in disgust. "That was just another ploy to gain your trust. He figured it was safe to tell you because you'd be dead and couldn't tell anyone. The bastard! He should be put behind bars, but we need proof before we can arrest him."

Andy was dismayed. "Richard, I know he did it! How else could the poison get into my system?"

"Wait until we see what the detective comes up with," Richard told her. "You get a good night's rest. And don't worry. We'll get this straightened out."

"Richard, is there any way to speed up this divorce? As long as Paul and I are married, he might try this again. Now that we know where Paul hid the money, there's no reason to wait, is there?"

"I'll see what I can do," Richard assured her.

CHAPTER XXIV

The next morning Paul was eating breakfast and listening to the news. The newscaster said Andy had already signed a contract for a television series of her novel. Filming was scheduled to start in two weeks. Her book was about to be translated into several languages to be sold in other countries. Not a word about her being in the hospital.

Guess it hasn't been reported yet, he figured. He wasn't worried. He had seen her being carried out of the hotel on a stretcher. That was good enough for him.

He smirked. She couldn't possibly survive. Not with what I put in her drink.

I couldn't have chosen a better time! he cheered. The television series and the foreign royalties could mean millions! And the house in Palos Verdes is worth at least three million!

I'm a rich man! I'm set for life!

The next two days he stuck close to the television, waiting for news of Andy's death. Someone at the Park Plaza had finally leaked the news to the media that she had been taken by ambulance to the hospital. Speculation had it that she had tried to commit suicide, but her condition was still a mystery.

Paul was getting impatient. How much longer do I have to wait? he fumed. I'm going to the hospital and find out what's going on.

He donned the silk, beige sport shirt and brown slacks he bought three days ago. To this outfit he added the off-white, silk knit sweater to complement the outfit. His beige loafers made the finishing touch. "You look like a million bucks!" he uttered out loud. "Just like the millions you'll soon be inheriting!"

He went down to the lobby and strode out the door, plotting just how he would finish Andy off.

There was a cab waiting at the curb, and he hopped in. No more subways for him! He arrived at the hospital and entered the building. As he walked up to the reception desk he did his best to look anxious and distraught. "Excuse me," he said to the nurse, "could you tell me which room Andora Jordan is in?"

"Oh, I'm sorry, Sir," she said, "but Mrs. Jordan isn't allowed any visitors. Doctor's orders."

Paul was prepared for this. "I'm her husband," he told the nurse. "How is she doing?"

The nurse hesitated. "How do I know you're not a reporter?"

"Oh, no," Paul replied. He reached for his wallet and held it up so she could see his picture with his identification.

"I'm sorry, Mr. Jordan," she apologized. "I was told to be careful. I haven't seen you here before."

"I've been out of town and just heard about this," he lied. "I would have been here much sooner if I'd known."

"Well - "The nurse hesitated. "I guess it's okay. Her room is number four-fifty-five on the fourth floor."

"Thank you."

Paul walked over and waited for the elevator.

But when the elevator door opened, Sonny got off.

Paul cursed under his breath as Sonny approached him. He tried to push past, but Sonny stopped him.

"Mr. Jordan," Sonny greeted him. "Andy isn't seeing anyone. I'm sorry. She's in no condition. She wouldn't even know you were there, so there's no point in your going up."

"How is she?" Paul asked.

"It doesn't look good," Sonny replied, shaking his head. "It's too bad. She just became a huge success, and now this."

Paul thought fast. "Well, I'd like to take a look at her," he said. "My presence might help."

"She needs rest and quiet," Sonny told him. "Look, why don't you and I have a cup of coffee. We can talk," he said, steering him away from the elevator and toward the exit.

Paul did his best not to show his annoyance. How am I going to get into her room and finish her off? he fumed. I've got to do something to speed things up.

But Sonny persisted. The next thing Paul knew he was in the coffee shop next door to the hospital and Sonny had ordered two cappuccinos.

Paul decided to make the best of it. "I've been quite worried about Andy," he said. "In spite of the pending divorce, I still care what happens to her."

Sonny remained poker faced. "Everything is being done to make her comfortable."

"What are her chances for recovery?" Paul asked.

Sonny looked grim. "It's very serious," he said. "The doctor doesn't hold out any hope." He shook his head. "No hope at all. She probably won't last another day."

"What a shame," Paul responded.

Guess there's no need for me to stick around, he mused. It won't be long now!

He looked at his watch. "I'd better get going," he told Sonny. "I have an appointment. Give her my love. They say people in a coma can hear what's going on. Tell her I'm praying for her." With that he left.

He silently cheered as he hailed a cab and went back to his elegant Park Avenue condo.

CHAPTER XXV

After a week's stay in the hospital, Andy had completely recovered, and was anxious to get on with her life. Her book was selling well even without her presence. The stores kept running out of copies and had to order more to keep up with the demand. Maddi and Sonny came to see her every day to keep her from getting bored, and to bring her clothes from the hotel.

The detective kept in touch with her on a regular basis. He had been able to confiscate the plastic bag from the waste basket in the men's room at the hotel, and although the contents had been poured out, there was enough left to be analyzed.

All Andy could do was wait.

It was late in the afternoon, and Andy was sitting in a chair reading the newspaper when the phone rang. She had been warned not to answer it. It might be a reporter who had heard rumors. Or even Paul, checking up on her.

Maddi and Sonny had just come over to visit, and Sonny picked up the phone. "Yes, who's calling? I see," Andy heard him say. "Very good. I'll tell her." He hung up and turned to Andy.

"Who was that?" she asked.

"The detective. He's on his way over. He just got the report from the lab."

"What did it say?" Maddi asked him.

"He didn't tell me. We'll have to wait until he gets here."

A half hour later the detective entered Andy's room.

"Did the lab find anything in the plastic bag?" she asked with mixed emotions. She held her breath, waiting for his answer.

The detective nodded. "Traces of the Margarita that were still in it match the poison found in your system. And your husband's fingerprints were on the glass and the bag. There's no doubt - he put that poison in your drink."

Andy was silent for a moment, digesting this. "Is it enough to arrest him?" she asked.

"There's more," the detective told her. "I questioned the bartender. He remembered seeing you in the lounge. He said you seemed perfectly normal when you came in, but when you left you were a bit unsteady on your feet. It puzzled him because all you had was that one Margarita, and you didn't finish that. He saw your husband put something into your drink. And he saw him dump the rest into the plastic bag after you left. He offered to testify. You have your proof, Mrs. Jordan."

For fully a minute Andy sat there, unable to move. As hard as she had prayed for proof, now that she had it, she felt sad at having to admit that Paul - her own husband - had actually tried to kill her. She had been hoping somewhere in the back of her mind that she was wrong, but she finally realized that for the past thirty years she had been living with a man who would stop at nothing - not even murder - to get what he wanted.

Without a word she walked over to the phone and dialed Richard's office in Los Angeles.

Richard answered when the call came through. "Yes, Andy," he said, "what's up?"

"We have the proof," Andy told him. "Paul really tried to kill me. There's no doubt." She told him what the detective had said.

"Is the detective there now?" Richard asked her. He sounded grim.

"Yes." She handed the phone to him and went back to her chair. She was shaking - partly from shock - partly from anger.

The detective talked briefly with Richard, and hung up. "I'm going back to the station and get a warrant for Paul Jordan's arrest," he told Andy. "Don't leave here until you hear from me. This is far from over."

"We'll stay with her," Maddi told him.

After the detective left, Maddi chided Andy. "You look sad. I would think you'd be relieved that this is finally being resolved. You won't have to stay here much longer."

Andy's eyes glistened with tears. "I guess something inside of me hates to admit that my own husband tried to kill me. I've doubted his love for a long time, but this - " her voice trailed off and she turned her head away.

Sonny went over and slipped his arm around her shoulder. "It's hard to find out that someone you trusted doesn't deserve that trust. But you have to put it behind you. You're alive, and you have a lot to look forward to."

"You need to get back to autographing your book," Maddi said. "As soon as we hear from the detective that Paul has been arrested, I'll make more appointments."

"Even if he gets out on bail, he wouldn't dare try anything else," Sonny promised. "You'll be safe. And think what crowds we'll get at the stores once the news hits the papers!"

Andy straightened her shoulders and stood up, shaking off the gloom. "I'll start packing. As soon as the detective says it's okay, I'm leaving the hospital. I'd better call Midge. I don't want it to come as a shock that her father - I mean, Paul - has been arrested. Thank God he's not her real father. That would really be hard to take."

"It might be wise not to go back to the hotel," Maddi suggested. "You can stay with me at my apartment. You'll be safe from reporters there."

"That's a great idea!" Sonny agreed. "That way we can keep an eye on you."

Andy nodded. "I'll call Midge and tell her."

There was no answer at Midge's condo in California. "She must still be with Jim in Santa Barbara," Andy said. She dialed Jim's number, and this time Midge answered on the first ring.

"Midge - " Andy barely got the words out of her mouth.

"Mom!" Midge exclaimed. "Are you okay? I tried several times to get you on the phone, but they said you weren't accepting any calls. Richard told me you were okay, and I should stay put."

"I'm just fine, dear. They were screening my calls to make sure no reporters got through. The reason I called - I wanted you to hear this from me, not from the news. We have proof positive that Paul tried to kill me. The detective went over to the police station a few minutes ago to get a warrant for his arrest. As soon as I hear he's in jail, I'm leaving here. I'll be staying with Maddi Seaford in her apartment." She gave Midge the phone number. "You can reach me there if you need me for anything."

Andy overheard Jim say, "Tell her to make sure she's safe."

Andy's heart skipped a beat. Is it too much to think that he still cares? Don't entertain any false hopes, she warned herself. "Tell him thanks," she told Midge. "I won't leave here until I'm sure. Have you set another date for your wedding?"

"Yes. John and I plan to be married on Christmas Day. I'll let you know the details. You have plenty of time to sign more books. I imagine when the public hears what happened you'll be mobbed. That's the only good thing that's come out of this mess. Take care of yourself, and keep in touch."

Andy ached with the desire to speak to Jim. But he didn't say anything, so she assumed that he still didn't believe her about the circumstances of Midge's paternity.

CHAPTER XXVI

Paul was alone in his condo when he heard a knock on the door. He looked through the peephole and saw a uniformed policeman standing there.

A feeling of uneasiness swept over him. "Who is it?" he asked.

"Police. Open up, please."

Paul opened the door. "What's the problem, officer?"

"Are you Paul Jordan?" the officer asked.

"Yes."

"We have a warrant for your arrest."

"What?! What for?!"

"Attempted murder."

Paul couldn't believe his ears! Attempted murder? Had he failed? Andy didn't die? She's still alive?

"You have the right to remain silent," the officer continued. "Anything you say can and will be used against you - "

"This is ridiculous!" Paul interrupted. "Who did I try to kill?"

"The warrant says you tried to kill your wife - Andy Jordan."

Paul searched quickly for the right words. "I never tried to kill anyone!" he declared vehemently. "Why would I try to kill my wife? Did she tell you this?"

"Mr. Jordan, you'd better not resist arrest. It will be that much harder on you."

Paul tried to shut the door, but the officer handcuffed him and led him to the elevator and down into the lobby.

"You can't do this to me!" Paul protested. "I don't deserve to be treated this way!"

The people in the lobby stared as the officer led him to the police car that was waiting outside. A reporter who had been standing by sped to the phone, anxious to be the first one to give his story to the press.

They soon arrived at the police station. "What about bail?" Paul asked. "I need a lawyer! Get me a lawyer!"

"You're allowed one call," he was told. "You can call him from the phone on the desk."

"I can't dial with these handcuffs on!" he shouted.

The officer removed the handcuffs. "Don't try to escape, Sir," he warned Paul. "I'll stand here while you make your call."

What Paul felt bordered on panic. The first thought that came to him was the fact that he didn't have a lawyer. The one he had hired to represent him in the divorce had deserted him. "I don't know who to call," he told the policeman.

"Surely there's someone," the officer said. "Someone in the family or a friend?"

With a shock Paul realized that he had no family or friends that he could call on to help him. It wouldn't do any good to call Andy - not after what he did to her. And he knew Richard wouldn't come to his defense. And Midge? Forget about her! He had no one.

The officer spoke to him sharply. "If you're not going to make a call, we'll have to lock you up. Make up your mind."

"I need a phone book," he said. His voice trembled.

"There's one beside the phone," the officer replied.

Paul's hands shook with fear as he picked it up and thumbed through the pages.

He finally found a list of lawyers and dialed one. "I've just been arrested for something I didn't do," he told the person on the other end. "I need a lawyer. Pronto! I'm at the police station in Greenwich Village."

"What's the charge?" the voice asked him.

"Attempted murder. I'm innocent, and I need a lawyer. Now!"

"What is your name, Sir?"

"Paul Jordan. I'm Andy Jordan's husband, and these charges are ridiculous!"

There was a long silence on the other end. Finally a man's voice came over the wire. "We'll send someone over right away."

The officer put the handcuffs back on Paul and led him away to a cell.

In half an hour the lawyer showed up, and Paul was taken into a private room.

"I'm Roy Wendell," the lawyer said extending his hand.

"I'm Paul Jordan, and I'm innocent!" Paul declared. "I don't know why they've arrested me! My wife is responsible for this!"

The lawyer waited until Paul had calmed down. "Now - tell me what happened and why you were arrested."

"I can't stay here," Paul mumbled. "You have to get me out of here."

"Mr. Jordan, there's nothing I can do until you tell me what happened."

"I'm being accused of poisoning my wife. She's in the hospital. I don't know who did this, but I didn't!"

"Which hospital is she in? I'll have to call and verify this."

"They'll only tell you lies!" Paul insisted. "I didn't do it, and that's all there is to it!"

"Where was this supposed to have taken place, Mr. Jordan?"

Paul calmed down enough to try and figure out what story he could make up that would sound plausible. "The cocktail lounge at the Park Plaza Hotel. My wife and I are getting a divorce. Now that my wife is a famous writer she thinks she's too good for me. I helped her every way I could when she started writing. I encouraged her - I did research - anything I could think of that would help her. Now she wants to dump me and take all the money. She knows I'll fight this, so she and her lawyer dreamed up this ridiculous accusation against me. They framed me!"

"If you're getting a divorce, how did you happen to be together at the hotel?"

Paul averted his eyes as he did some quick thinking. What will convince him that Andy is the guilty party?

"She called me the other night and asked me to meet her there for a farewell drink," he lied. "She must have slipped the poison into her own drink when I wasn't looking. Then she went up to her room and called the ambulance before she passed out. I don't know if she's still at the hospital or not. They wouldn't let me see her. I'm being framed! Can't you get me out on bail? I don't belong here!"

"I'll see what I can do," the lawyer told him.

"I'm subletting a condo on Park Avenue. I'm afraid with the publicity that they'll rent it to someone else."

"I'll take care of that," the lawyer assured him. "What is the address?" He jotted it down. "I'll be in touch," he told Paul.

The policeman let him out and took Paul back to his cell.

CHAPTER XXVII

As soon as the detective notified Andy at the hospital that Paul had been arrested, she put on her jacket and grabbed her purse and suitcase. "Come on," she said to Maddi and Sonny, "we're out of here."

"Hold on!" Sonny admonished her. "There are bound to be reporters hanging around the lobby." He picked up the phone. "I'll call for a limo and tell them to meet us at the back entrance in ten minutes. We'll wait here and go down the back way."

The guard who had been posted outside the door poked his head into the room. "They tell me I'm no longer needed here, so I'll be leaving. It's been a pleasure." He hesitated. "Uh - Mrs. Jordan, you don't happen to have an extra copy of your book, do you? My wife would love to have an autographed copy. She was thrilled when I told her I was assigned to guard you. She loves your book."

Sonny reached into his briefcase and handed the book to Andy, who promptly signed it. Her life was finally getting back to normal.

"Hey - thanks!" The guard took it, donned his visored cap, and left.

In ten minutes Sonny rose and ushered Andy and Maddie to the back elevator. The limousine was waiting outside the back entrance.

Sonny rushed Andy into the limo just as the reporters came running around the corner. They chased the car shouting questions. The driver gunned the accelerator, leaving eager reporters behind. How did they know? Andy wondered.

In twenty minutes the limousine arrived at Maddi's condo. No reporters there. They made their way to the elevator and pressed the button for the tenth floor.

As they entered the condo the view of the East River could be seen through the picture windows. It was a clear day and the sunlight sparkled on the water. A sightseeing boat loaded with passengers sailed by. What a welcome relief this was to Andy, who for the past week had had only the grey walls of her hospital room to stare at.

The tasteful furnishings of the condo were done in the French Provincial style of Louis XIV. The divan facing the large picture window was upholstered in white silk with small flecks of blue and peach, and the chairs on either side were covered in a peach color with a blue border. The drapes were a beautiful French blue, matching the blue border on the chairs. Added to this were peach colored tie-backs. On the hardwood floors were Oriental rugs with hues that blended in with the colors of the upholstery and the drapes. What a beautiful home! Andy marveled.

As soon as Andy's suitcase was placed in the spare bedroom, Maddi switched on the television to get the news which was coming up shortly.

"There's a Chinese restaurant around the corner," Sonny said. "How does Chinese take-out sound, Andy?"

"After hospital food it sounds like heaven! Let's go for it!" she said as she made herself comfortable on the sofa.

The food arrived in just under twenty minutes. As they ate, the news came on. Andy's picture was on the screen, and the newscaster was having a heyday with speculations.

"Breaking news!" he announced. "Author Andy Jordan was just released from the hospital. No one seems to know the story behind her illness. The report is that she overdosed on sleeping pills, but there is some question about that. It's a big mystery. Her husband has been arrested on a charge of attempted murder. Did he try to murder his own wife? If so, why? Stay tuned for later developments."

"We've got to set them straight!" Maddi declared. "We can't have them believing you tried to kill yourself. Now that Paul has been arrested, we should tell the news media the truth."

"Maybe we should set up a news conference with the press," Sonny suggested.

Andy disagreed. "You'd better check with the detective first," she warned. "If this were to hit the papers before Paul has a chance for a fair trial it would be hard to find an unbiased jury. I'd hate to see him get off scot free on a technicality."

They finished eating, and Andy walked over to the window. The lights were just coming on. She had come to love these lights in the skyscrapers and she felt reluctant to leave her new exciting life here in New York City. But she also felt the need to return to the peace and quiet of her lovely home in California.

After contemplating this for a few moments, she turned back to Maddi and Sonny. "I think I should go home. No one knows where I live and no one can call me. I have an unlisted number. I'll be safe from reporters there. My book will sell whether I'm here to sign it or not. If I appeared at the bookstore now, I'd be swamped with people asking questions. I'm not sure how much I should tell them."

Sonny nodded. "You're right. We'll have to think of a way to smuggle you out of here without anyone knowing."

"An early flight would be the answer," Maddi stated.

Sonny picked up the phone and dialed the airline. "What's your earliest flight to Los Angeles tomorrow morning?" he asked the ticket agent. He waited. "Good! Please book a seat for -" he paused - - "Maddi Seaford in First Class. Charge it to Maddison Publications. Thank you." He hung up. "This will keep your name out of it," he told Andy. "We'll go with you to the airport, and Maddi will pick up your ticket so no one will know it's for you. Let's hope you can go incognito all the way. The flight leaves at five-forty-five. The limo will pick you up here at four o'clock in the morning. Wear dark glasses and pull your coat collar up around your face so no one will recognize you."

"What time does the plane get in?" Andy asked him.

"Seven-thirty in the morning, California time."

"I'll call Midge and have her meet me," Andy said.

Sonny put on his coat and headed for the door. "I'd better get going," he said. He turned back to Andy. "Just in case Paul manages to get out on bail, you'd better change the locks in your house. And change the code on your alarm system. I'll see you at four o'clock in the morning. Go to bed and get a good night's sleep. Both of you. We'll be up before the chickens."

He left, and Maddi and Andy retired for the night.

CHAPTER XXVIII

Andy's plane arrived in Los Angeles a little early. The flight was smooth and uneventful. No one recognized her except for the flight attendant who was discreet enough to keep quiet.

Midge was waiting at the gate. Andy half hoped that Jim might be there, but Midge was alone.

As much as Andy had come to love New York with its frenzied activity and dazzling lights, she was delighted to be in her own home once more with its peace and quiet, and her beautiful view of the ocean. The steady pounding of the waves as they rolled in and hit the shore was music to her ears.

The first thing she did before she unpacked was to call her neighbor, Jerry Pacheco, a building contractor who lived across the street. When he did the addition on her home ten years ago he had installed all new doors and windows throughout the house, and was familiar with the latches on the doors. He promised to be there in twenty minutes with his equipment to change the locks.

Andy looked at her watch. Eight-thirty in the morning. While she waited for Jerry, she changed the code on the security alarm.

She couldn't imagine Paul being able to obtain bail, but he had done a lot of things that seemed impossible, and she knew Sonny was right. She should take all precautions.

"I'm staying with you tonight," Midge announced. "Dad told me to make sure you were safe."

Andy's hopes rose again. She squelched it. No, she decided, I'm not going to read something into this that's not there.

It wasn't long before her neighbor finished changing the locks, and Andy had a new key. "Good!" she said. She thanked Jerry and told him to send her a bill.

As soon as he left, she turned to Midge. "I'm hungry. How about going out for an early lunch? There's nothing in the house, and I feel like trying that new restaurant on the ocean. What's the name? - - Dolphin Cove West! I saw an ad in the magazine on the plane, and it said the food was wonderful. It's early, so we should be in and out before the lunch crowd arrives."

Midge gazed lovingly at her mother. "I'm glad to see you're back to your old self again. You had Dad and me worried."

"Well, that's all over now. I'm fine, and Paul is behind bars. I only hope he stays there."

"You think he won't?"

Andy shrugged. "With him you never know. Let's go! I'm starved! You drive," she said to Midge, handing her the keys. "I was up at three this morning with only four hours sleep. I might doze off."

The top was down on her Jaguar convertible. She was still wearing her comfortable blue jeans and sweat shirt she had learned to wear when she traveled on the plane. She threw her white London Fog jacket around her shoulders, donned her visored cap, put on her dark glasses, and she and Midge headed for Dolphin Cove West.

The restaurant was just twelve miles down the road, and they arrived at ten o'clock, well before the lunch crowd was due. The maitre d' seated them at a secluded table by a window that looked out on the channel, as Midge requested.

"I'm going to have the seafood salad," Andy told Midge. "Would you order for me? I don't want anyone to know I'm here. They'll ask a lot of questions I can't answer."

"Sure, Mom," Midge agreed.

Andy gazed out the window, hiding her face from the waiter.

As soon as he left, Midge turned to her mother with an amused look on her face. "Vive la being a celebrity! It's not all it's cracked up to be, is it? Your privacy is kaput!"

Andy laughed. "You can say that again!" Then on a more sober tone she asked, "How was your visit with Jim?"

Midge's face glowed. "Mom, it was the best ever! I've waited twenty-nine years for a Dad who loved me. And he really does. I'm so grateful every day that he's my father. I couldn't ask for anyone nicer."

"I'm glad, dear. I only wish - " she stopped in mid-sentence.

"Wish what, Mom?"

"Oh," she sighed, "I wish he had believed me when I told him I didn't know you were his daughter."

"He does, Mom. He told me so."

"Oh? Well, I guess that's not enough. He hasn't tried to get in touch with me."

Midge shook her head. "You two are a pair, you know that? He's afraid to call - you're afraid to call - what am I going to do with you two?"

Andy lowered her eyes and stared at the table. "I think if he really wanted to call he would," she mumbled.

Midge changed the subject. "Let's talk about the wedding. You haven't asked me about any of the details."

"Oh, I'm sorry, dear. I've had a lot on my mind. It's not easy finding out your husband of thirty years tried to kill you. I've known for a long time that there's no love lost between Paul and me, but - "

Midge reached out and squeezed Andy's hand. "I know, Mom. But you've got to put all that behind you."

"That's what Sonny said, but I can't help feeling sad about the whole thing." She shook it off. "Enough about me. Tell me your plans. Are you going to be married in a church?"

Midge's eyes twinkled and her face lit up. "If you don't mind," she said, "John and I would love to be married on the terrace in your back yard overlooking the ocean. We can't think of a better place. It will be so special."

Andy was delighted! The terrace, protected by a white, wrought iron fence bordering the ocean, was unique - big enough to seat at least seventy people. The floor was tiled with black and white ceramic squares. Great for parties, and certainly for such a festive occasion as a wedding!

"Oh, honey," she exclaimed, "that's just perfect! It's big enough to set up chairs, and there's even room for an aisle!"

As the waiter arrived with their lunch, Andy looked out and saw a huge ocean liner sail past the window on its way to the open sea. Nostalgia gripped her as she struggled to hold back the tears. Wonderful memories flooded her thoughts. It seemed like just yesterday that she and Jim had sailed around the world together.

Forget it. That's all in the past.

As she and Midge ate, the luncheon crowd began to arrive, and the place was filling up fast. Andy hoped no one would recognize her. That would defeat the very reason she had returned to California. She was looking forward to getting back to the house and working on her new novel. Ideas were dancing around in her head, and she couldn't wait to store them in her computer.

Up to now Andy had remained incognito, but as they finished their delicious lunch and rose to leave, one of the customers spotted her.

"Andy Jordan! I thought I recognized you! I've seen your picture on the jacket of your book! Tell me," she gushed in a loud voice, "did your husband really try to murder you? How awful! You should write about it in your next novel!" She took a small pad of paper and a pen out of her purse. "Could I have your autograph?"

Midge stepped in and put a stop to it. "What makes you think this is Andy Jordan?" she asked. "Don't you know everyone has a look-alike?" She rushed Andy out of the restaurant and to the car as fast as she could, jumped in behind the wheel, and drove away.

Andy was grateful. "I'm glad you were with me. I wouldn't have known what to do."

Midge's jaw was set as she used to do when she was a little girl. "What's the matter with people? That was downright rude!" She drove a little faster than usual. "We'll get you home right away," she told Andy. "Then I'm going to the store and get plenty of food so you won't have to go out for a while."

Andy grimaced. "I guess I'm going to be a prisoner in my own home. I can't seem to escape it. Oh, well," she continued, trying to look on the positive side, "that will give me plenty of time to work on my new book."

As Midge drove Andy's car into the garage they heard the phone ringing. Andy rushed to answer it.

It was Richard. "Ready for some good news?" he asked her.

"I could use some right now," Andy replied. "What's up?"

"I just heard from one of the judges in Superior Court in New York. They plan to hold Paul's preliminary hearing next month."

"Oh! That's wonderful, Richard," Andy exclaimed.

"I just wanted to let you know. Don't worry about a thing. There's no way Paul can get out of this one!"

"I'll be glad when this whole rotten mess is over," Andy said. "Thanks, Richard."

The following month Andy did little else than work on her new book.

One or two nights a week Midge and John came over to keep her company so she wouldn't feel too shut out from the world. She didn't think it was wise to expose herself again to public scrutiny.

She had made a big mistake going to Dolphin Cove West for lunch. She may have avoided reporters, but she brought herself face to face with people's morbid curiosity. *I won't make that mistake again!* she vowed. *Thank God Midge was with me. I could easily have said something that would have ruined the upcoming hearing.*

She was ready to testify. So were Maddi and Sonny, and the detective who uncovered the evidence. Even Richard said he'd testify if necessary.

Her divorce hearing was due to come up in California soon, and she prayed that it would go through without a hitch. Paul would be unable to attend, but Richard said it didn't matter. After what Paul did to her he didn't anticipate any problem. They fully expected that Paul would be behind prison bars for a number of years.

The day finally came for the divorce hearing. Andy rose early, ready to appear before the judge in Los Angeles. Midge would be meeting her there and testifying on her behalf. Richard was expected any minute to drive her into the city.

It was a private hearing in the judge's chambers. After hearing all the evidence against Paul, and Midge's testimony, the judge made a decision. "Divorce granted," Andy heard him say. "There will be a two month waiting period before it becomes final on December fifteen."

After thanking Midge and saying goodbye, Andy walked out of the judge's chambers. In just two months she would be a free woman. Now all she had to be concerned with was Paul's hearing.

"Richard, thank you," she said as they walked toward the car in the parking lot outside the Municipal Building. "I can't thank you enough. I feel as though I just dropped a ton. I didn't realize until now how this whole thing has been weighing me down."

As she got into the car she saw some reporters headed in their direction. "Richard - " she said in a panic. Richard jumped in behind the wheel, started the engine, and gunned the accelerator. They left the parking lot with tires screeching and reporters running after them, bombarding them with questions.

As soon as they escaped into traffic Richard turned to Andy. "I'm taking you to my private club here in the city," he told her. "No one is allowed except members and guests. We'll have a nice quiet lunch and celebrate. We've just gone over a hugh hurdle today."

Andy smiled at him, deeply grateful. "What would I do without your help?" she said. "You've been a Rock of Gilbralter these last few months."

Richard grinned. "Wait until you get my bill," he teased.

Andy laughed. She felt almost lighthearted again, even with Paul's impending hearing hanging over her.

Richard drove the car up to the parking valet, and he and Andy got out. As they entered the brownstone building, the soft strains of Chopin could be heard. The maitre d' ushered them to a table beside the fireplace - a welcome warmth in contrast to the cooling of the early autumn air outside. The room was very much like one of the English Pubs that Andy had visited on one of the stops the cruise ship made. Rich carpet graced the floor, and dark mahogany panels covered the walls. Again she was reminded of Jim.

She and Richard were early and had the place to themselves. The music was soothing. All that invaded the peace and harmony of the room was the sound of the crackling fire. It seemed like heaven to Andy not having to worry about any reporters hounding her with their zest for scandal.

The waiter approached them, and Richard ordered two White Zinfandels with a twist of lemon.

"You remembered!" Andy said. "It's been - what - two years since we've been together socially?"

"It was fun, wasn't it?" Richard mused. "Until Paul spoiled it. But that's in the past. Andy, I'm so proud of you. You've come a long way since then. You're a whole person."

"Thanks, Richard. Coming from you that's quite a compliment." The drinks were on the table, and Andy lifted her glass. "Shall we toast to that?"

Richard raised his glass in reply. They sat in silence, studying the menu and sipping their wine. Soon the peace and quiet was interrupted by more guests arriving. If any of them recognized Andy they didn't show it, and she relaxed. Paul's hearing was a week away, but right now she decided she was just going to enjoy the here and now, and worry about that later.

CHAPTER XXIX

Paul sat in his cell alone and angry. Almost a month had passed by since his lawyer had been back to the jail. He called Paul a couple of times and said he was busy investigating what he told him, but he was running into some snags and it was taking longer than he had anticipated.

Paul was still sulking when he was told he had a visitor. He was led into the private room where the lawyer was waiting.

"Where have you been?" Paul asked. "You certainly took your time! Are you getting me out of here?"

Roy Wendell ignored Paul's remarks. "I've looked into this thoroughly," he told him. "All the evidence points to you, and says you're guilty as hell. However, everyone is entitled to a fair trial. Your wife is still alive, so you didn't actually commit murder. I'll take the case, but only if you'll agree to do exactly as I say."

"I'll do anything it takes to get out of here!" Paul vowed.

"I want you to plead innocent. You say you did everything to encourage your wife with her writing? A judge would be sympathetic if he thought she was about to cast you aside with nothing now that she's a success. Since you claim that she put the poison into her own drink, we'll try and convince him that she tried to frame you."

Paul breathed a sigh of relief. "Is my wife still in the hospital?" he asked.

"No, she left the hospital the day you were arrested, and went back to California the next day."

Paul clenched his fists in anger. How can I get out of here and take care of Andy with her three thousand miles away? he fumed silently.

"Do you really think this will work?" he asked the lawyer.

"We can only try. It's the best shot we have."

"Okay," Paul agreed. "Let's go for it."

"Do you have any previous record?"

"Absolutely not!" Paul declared.

The lawyer nodded. "I'll see what I can do," he promised. "I'll let you know as soon as I find out."

"How long do you think it will take? I don't want to spend another night in jail."

"I'll speak to the judge right away, and maybe have you out by late afternoon. Hang tight. I'll get back to you."

It was six o'clock in the evening when Paul's lawyer finally appeared at the cell door with a policeman. "Come on," he said. "You're out of here. I finally convinced the judge that until the hearing you haven't been formally charged with anything. You're being released on your own recognizance on one condition. You're to stay here in New York City until the trial. If you leave to go anywhere else, you'll be arrested and brought back here. Is that understood?"

"I won't leave the city," Paul vowed.

He would have agreed to anything to get out of jail, whether or not he intended to keep his word.

When he arrived at the condo, there was mail to be sorted out. One letter had Richard's return address on it.

He opened it and cursed.

The letter informed him that his and Andy's divorce would be final on December fifteen.

He had to take care of Andy before then. Otherwise, it would be too late. He would get nothing.

No community property.

No royalties from her book.

Nothing.

He sat down to figure out his next move. His mind was in a turmoil. I can't wait until the trial is over. That would be too late! December fifteen will be long gone by then. And as long as Andy is alive I don't stand a chance of staying out of jail.

There's only one answer. I have to get to California and kill her.

But how do I get there without the authorities knowing I left New York?

Disguise!

That's the key word!

But how?

What?

Then he remembered! One of the shops across the street from his condo sold wigs and beards. A grey wig and beard! That's it! He raced down to the lobby and walked over to the shop. In less than twenty minutes he found what he was looking for, and was back in his condo. He took the wig and beard out of the package and put them on.

As he walked over to the mirror he was startled. For a split second he thought someone else was in the room. Then he realized it was his own image! He looked so different it fooled even him! This plus dark glasses he knew without a doubt would complete his disguise!

But what if the authorities should decide to check up on me? How will I fool them into thinking I'm still here in New York? After pondering some more, he came up with what seemed to be a foolproof plan.

He picked up the phone and called the reception desk. "I don't want any calls or visitors for the next two days," he told the security guard. "If anyone comes here to see me, please tell them I'm working on a book, and can't be disturbed."

"Yes, Sir," the guard promised. "I won't let anyone come up to your room."

Next, Paul recorded a message on the answering machine he had bought when he first came to New York. On it he taped the following message:

"Hello. I don't want to be disturbed. I'm writing a book. Please call later." Then the sound of the phone hanging up and a dial tone. Whoever called would think he had answered the phone himself.

He had enough cash in his wallet for a cab to the airport and the cheapest ticket on the plane. He called the airport. "When is your next plane to Los Angeles?" he asked when the ticket agent came on the line.

"The Red Eye leaves at twelve-forty-five, and gets in at twelve-forty-five tomorrow morning, California time," she informed him.

Paul did some quick figuring. That puts me at the house in Palos Verdes by one-thirty in the morning - plenty of time to do away with Andy and get to the airport for an early flight back to New York! "Please book me on that flight," he said.

"What is your name, Sir?"

Paul groped for a phony name that no one could check on. "Peter Jenkins," he told her.

"Yes, Mr. Jenkins. Is this one way or round trip, Sir?"

"Round trip. Book me on the three AM flight coming back tomorrow morning."

"Yes, Sir. You're all booked. Please be here an hour before departure and pick up your ticket."

Paul didn't pack anything. This way, if anyone checked up on him, they would find his clothes and his suitcase still in the closet. It won't take long to take care of Andy. The three o'clock flight from Los Angeles to New York will land at five o'clock tomorrow morning, New York time. I'll grab a cab and be back in my condo by six!

No one will guess that I went to California! he exulted.

This will work!

I know it will!

It has to!

He adjusted his wig, checked the beard, changed to jeans and a tee shirt, donned his dark glasses, and rang for the elevator. He walked across the lobby without being noticed.

Once outside, he flagged down a cab and was on his way to Kennedy Airport and California.

CHAPTER XXX

It was ten o'clock at night. Andy was tired and just about to retire when the phone rang. Who can that be at this time of night? she wondered.

It was Richard. "Andy, I hate to tell you this, but I just got a call from Superior Court in New York. They tell me Paul has been released until the hearing. He must have a smart lawyer. Please be careful. Be sure your house alarm is set."

Andy's heart pounded with fear. "I thought the evidence was airtight." Her voice trembled. "I had the locks changed. There's no way he can get in."

"He can if he breaks a window," Richard warned her. "That's why it's so important to set your house alarm. You're connected with the police department, aren't you?"

"Yes. The alarm is already set. If anyone breaks in, the police will be here in five minutes."

"I wonder just how wise it is for you to be in the house alone. Do you think you should call Midge and ask her to come over?"

"I don't want to call her and ask her to drive all the way here this late at night," Andy told him. "We're not even sure Paul will come to California. Doesn't he have to stay in New York? I thought there would be restrictions on where he could go."

"Oh, he's been told to stay in New York until the hearing or he'll be back in jail, but you know Paul. He's pretty slick. You can't be too careful, Andy."

"I'll call you first thing in the morning," she promised him. "I'm sure I'll be okay."

She hung up, not as sure of her safety as she sounded. Before climbing into bed she locked her bedroom door. But as much as she needed to rest, she was afraid to fall asleep.

She tossed and turned, unable to allay the fear that crept into her thought. What if Paul does come to California? No, that's not possible. He wouldn't take the chance that he might be caught. She dozed off and on, looking now and then at the clock. She finally turned on the small television set in the bedroom. By this time it was one o'clock in the morning, and the channel she tuned to had a recap of the day's news.

"Paul Jordan, Andy Jordan's husband, was released under his own recognizance late yesterday afternoon," she heard the announcer say.

That much she knew, but she was shocked at the report that followed.

"There is some doubt," the announcer continued, "that there is any merit to the accusation that he was responsible for the poison found in his wife's drink. Word has it that they're in the process of getting a divorce, and he claims that she put the substance into her own drink in an effort to frame him for attempted murder. He says she and her lawyer cooked up this scheme so he wouldn't get any kind of settlement from her. We'll keep you updated as we get more information."

"That's a lie!" Andy gasped.

She turned off the television and lay there, stunned. Her first impulse was to call Richard. But it was three hours ago that he had called her, and she was sure he would be asleep by now. She decided it could wait until morning.

As she pondered this she heard a sound coming from the basement.

She waited.

Listened.

Nothing more.

But she wasn't taking any chances.

She jumped out of bed and grabbed her robe. Her thoughts raced. Why didn't I call Midge and ask her to come over?

Her heart picked up speed. I have to get out of here!

As she headed toward the door, she heard footsteps coming up the stairs from the basement.

Then she remembered! Paul still had the old key! Only three locks in the house had been changed!

The lock on the door that led into the cellar hadn't been touched! The door was never used, and she had forgotten all about it. That door had never been connected to the alarm system! The cellar could be entered without triggering the alarm, but only someone familiar with the house would know that.

It has to be Paul! she thought in a panic.

She rushed to the phone to call the police.

No dial tone!

She looked toward the door and saw the knob turn. Sheer terror overwhelmed her. How did Paul get here from New York without being caught?

The door shook.

He was trying to force it open!

It wouldn't budge.

Just as she turned to run into the bathroom, the door burst from its hinges and Paul pushed his way into the room.

Andy screamed as he lunged toward her and put his hand over her mouth to stifle any sound.

She tried to fight him off, but he grabbed a pillow from the bed and held it over her face.

She gasped for breath. As her air was cut off she felt dizzy and lightheaded.

The last thing she remembered was the sensation of her knees buckling under her as she went down.

When she came to she was in her own bed. An oxygen mask was over her face, and a paramedic was bending over her. She heard sirens, and when she turned her head and looked out the window, she saw cars with flashing lights, and several policemen running around.

Paul, in handcuffs, was being led to one of the police cars.

Andy tore off the mask. "What happened?" she asked.

"You're going to be fine," the paramedic told her. "Just take it easy."

"How did you get here?" she asked as her memory floated back to her. "I tried to call the police, but the phone was dead."

One of the policemen came over to her bed. "Mrs. Jordan," he said, "you can thank your neighbor, Mr. Pacheco. He heard you scream and called us. He was waiting here with a key to let us in. Your lawyer had alerted us that something like this might happen, and one of our men was already here patrolling the neighborhood when the call came in. We got here just in time. Your husband tried to smother you with your pillow. He ran out the back door when he heard the siren. We found him hiding in some bushes. We're taking him back to New York. He won't get out of jail again."

Andy struggled to sit up. "What time is it?"

"Three o'clock in the morning," the paramedic told her. "I'm going to give you something to help you sleep. I've checked with your doctor and he okayed the medication. There's nothing to worry about now, and you need some rest. Mr. Pacheco said he'd fix your bedroom door tomorrow."

"Please," she said as the paramedic handed her a mild sedative and a glass of water, "I have to call my daughter and my lawyer. I don't want them hearing this on the news. It would be a terrible shock."

"I'll call them," he assured her. "Just tell me where you keep the names and phone numbers."

Andy pointed toward the drawer of the night stand beside her bed.

She drifted off to sleep.

It was noon when she woke up.

Midge was sitting by her bedside. She smiled when Andy opened her eyes. "Hi," she greeted her. "I thought you were going to sleep all day. Are you hungry?"

Andy sat up in bed and looked around. "Has Paul gone?"

"The police sent him back to New York with a guard to make sure he didn't escape," she assured Andy. "He won't be bothering you any more."

Andy could feel her whole body relax. "I guess this will convince the judge to hold him over for trial."

"Do you feel like getting up?" Midge asked.

Andy threw back the covers. She felt as though the weight of the world had dropped from her. "Did Richard call?"

"Yes," Midge replied. "He said he had something to tell you. He'll be here in about fifteen minutes. I'll have lunch ready by the time he gets here, and he'll eat with us. Get dressed. I'll see you in the kitchen," she said and left.

By the time Richard rang the doorbell Andy was dressed and anxious to hear what he had to say.

"Andy!" he exclaimed. "How are you feeling? You look great!"

"Come into the kitchen," she told him. "Midge has lunch ready. What is it that you have to tell me?"

"Great news, Andy! I found the five hundred thousand dollars that Paul took. It's all there in the Cayman Islands. They have orders to release it to you now that Paul is in jail. In view of all that happened he won't get one red cent. They'll be transferring the whole amount plus the interest into your bank account here in Palos Verdes."

Andy breathed a big sigh of relief. "Thank you, Richard. I can't believe this nightmare is almost over." She reached into the refrigerator and took out a bottle of champagne. "This calls for a celebration." She opened the bottle and poured the champagne into three flutes. "Here's to the future!" she toasted.

She was free of Paul, and her divorce would be final in a month. She was grateful to be alive and ready to face a whole new world.

How she wished it could be with Jim!

CHAPTER XXXI

Andy's second novel was half finished when she was summoned to testify at Paul's hearing. She and Richard planned to fly to New York together, and be at the courthouse early the next morning. Midge, who was still staying with Andy, was told it wasn't necessary to appear as a witness. The evidence spoke for itself.

"You stay here and plan your wedding," Andy told her. "It's coming up in less than two weeks. You have plenty to do. Richard and I will handle things at the hearing."

"I hope it doesn't take too long," Midge said. "You have to be back here for my wedding."

"I'll be here," she assured her. "Richard says with all the evidence against Paul it shouldn't take long for the judge to decide to hold him over for trial. Don't worry. I wouldn't want you to postpone the wedding again."

Andy thought she sensed an unusual urgency in Midge's voice. She remembered seeing that same look in her eyes when she was a child and had a secret surprise planned.

What is she up to now? she wondered.

She schemed to have Jim on the same cruise I was on.

Now what?

You're imagining things, she told herself, and quickly dismissed it.

When Richard arrived to drive Andy to the airport he handed her a document. "Here, Andy," he said, "sign this. It will make the divorce final."

Andy was surprised. "I thought all the details had been taken care of."

"This is the last document," Richard told her.

She didn't hesitate to sign it. The sooner it's over the better! It was December thirteen. In two days she would be single again!

Andy and Richard were at the courthouse in New York at nine o'clock the next morning.

As Paul was brought in by the guard, he looked in Andy's direction, a hurt expression on his face.

Andy stared back. She knew he was trying to play on her sympathy, but all she could feel was contempt. He was getting exactly what he deserved after trying twice to kill her.

The judge entered the courtroom, and the hearing began.

Richard called Andy to the stand and she was sworn in.

After a short interrogation by him, Roy Wendell, Paul's lawyer, walked over to her.

He stood silently for a few moments and stared at her, but Andy refused to be jarred by this tactic.

"Mrs. Jordan, you're a well known writer, aren't you?"

"Yes," Andy answered.

"It must have been frustrating trying to get a publisher, wasn't it?"

Andy shrugged. "It took a few months."

"Really? Your book must have been in pretty good shape then. Is that correct?"

"Yes."

"Tell me, Mrs. Jordan, who did your research and editing?"

Andy was surprised at his question. "I did," she told him.

"Oh? That's strange. Your husband, the defendant, tells me he did everything to help you, including research and editing. Isn't that true?"

Andy was indignant. "Certainly not!" she declared. "He never lifted a finger to help me!"

"Are you sure?" the lawyer asked her.

Andy glared at Paul as she answered the lawyer's question. "He did everything to discourage me! He told me it took a special kind of person with talent to write, and I wasn't one of them!"

"Mrs. Jordan, if he did everything to discourage you from writing, as you say, how does it happen that you now have a best seller in the book stores? Isn't he the one who sent your novel to the publisher for consideration?"

Andy couldn't believe her ears. What a liar Paul is! she fumed.

She waited until she was composed enough to answer calmly. "He didn't send it. I did. He didn't even know I'd written it."

"Oh, come now, Mrs. Jordan. How could he not know if you were living in the same house together?"

Andy gave him an icy stare. "Paul wasn't there. He came to me months ago and told me wanted an open marriage. I wanted no part of it. He left and came to New York, and I went on a cruise. That was when I found the time to finish a novel I'd started twenty-eight years ago. He wasn't there to interfere. The Purser on the ship told me about a publisher who was looking for new material. I sent it from one of the ports where the ship docked. Paul was in New York and knew nothing about it."

Roy Wendell quickly changed to another line of questioning. "Oh, yes. The cruise. I understand you took that cruise with an old boy friend. Isn't it true that he was the real father of your daughter? And you never bothered to tell your husband that he wasn't the father?"

"I object to this line of questioning!" Richard interrupted. "It's totally irrelevant to the case! My client is not on trial! Her husband is, for trying twice to murder her!"

"Your Honor," Paul's lawyer continued, "my client claims that his wife tried to frame him so she wouldn't have to give him a settlement in their pending divorce. The only reason he went to California where this alleged attempt at murder was supposed to have taken place was to try and reason with her - "

The judge banged his gavel. "The objection is sustained," he said. "Your client disobeyed the order not to leave town. Please get on with the questioning."

"Yes, Your Honor." He turned to Andy. "Would you please explain why you didn't tell your husband that he wasn't the father of your child?"

Andy tried to remain calm. "I didn't tell him because I didn't know."

Roy Wendell pointed an accusing finger at her. "Remember, Mrs. Jordan, you're under oath."

"I'm glad you asked that question," she snapped. "Now I can tell you what really happened. I didn't know until two months ago when my daughter needed a transfusion. My husband's blood didn't match, and neither did mine. There was only one other person who could be her father, and that's when I found out. After I married Paul I never looked at another man. I had no idea then that I was pregnant. I thought Midge was a premie."

Richard stood up and addressed the judge. "I wish to testify, Your Honor. May I be sworn in?"

Andy saw Paul gesture wildly to his lawyer and shake his head in an attempt to keep Richard from testifying.

The judge eyed Paul and came to a quick decision.

"Please swear this man in," he said. "I'm sure he has something important to say."

The bailiff told Richard to hold out his hand. "Do you promise to tell the truth, the whole truth, and nothing but the truth, so help you God?"

"I do!" Richard declared.

As soon as he was seated, the judge turned to him. "Mr. Ingalls, what is it that you have to say?"

"Your Honor, Mrs. Jordan is telling the truth. Paul was the unfaithful one. He had an affair with my wife and broke up my marriage." He looked at Paul. "You've got some nerve accusing Andy of being unfaithful to you! You left her so you could fool around with other women; you tried twice to kill her so you'd get all the money she made with her writing; you cleaned out your joint bank account - half a million dollars - and hid it from her in an illegal account in the Cayman Islands; and you spent money like Niagara Falls and left her with nothing to pay all your horrendous bills!"

"That's a pack of lies!" Paul yelled. He turned to the judge. "Andy put poison into her own drink and tried to frame me! When that didn't work, she tried to kill herself when I went to California to reason with her! Just another attempt to frame me!"

Richard glared at him, then burst out laughing at the ridiculousness of the accusation. "Paul, how could she smother herself with her own pillow?" He stopped laughing and turned to the judge with a stern look. "There's something else you should know, Your Honor. I didn't want to mention it, but now I have no choice. When Andy's daughter was only sixteen, the defendant tried to molest her. She was forced to move into her own apartment when she was old enough, just to avoid him."

This shocking news set off an uproar in the courtroom.

The judge banged his gavel again. "Order! Order in the court!" he demanded. He turned to Paul's lawyer. "Do you have anything further to say in defense of your client?"

"Not at this time, Your Honor." A stunned lawyer sat down and glared at Paul. "You weren't honest with me," he whispered.

"You may step down," the judge told Richard. He turned to Paul's lawyer. "This is the most ridiculous travesty of justice I have ever encountered in all my years on the bench. Unless you have witnesses to call, or something else to say in defense of this man, I will adjourn for the day."

Roy Wendell looked confused. "Your Honor, I have nothing further to say until I discuss this with my client."

The judge banged his gavel. "Court will reconvene tomorrow morning at nine o'clock."

Richard rose and went over to Andy. "How about some lunch?"

Andy's stomach was jumping up and down like a yoyo. "I don't think I can eat anything," she told him.

Richard took her hand and pulled her up. "Come on," he said. "I'm buying. I think a soothing glass of wine will settle you down. I know a cozy place around the corner from here. It's secluded, so no one will bother us. They have wonderful food. I'm sure you can eat a little something."

Andy donned her dark glasses and followed him. Once they were seated in the cafe she felt better. The wine that Richard ordered relaxed her stomach. The light salad she ordered was just what she needed, and she was ready to go back to the hotel and rest.

By nine o'clock the next morning they were back in court. The judge called Roy Wendell and Richard to the bench. "Do you have any witnesses or anything further to say?" he asked.

"Your Honor, I think you've heard everything that Mrs. Jordan has to say," Richard told him.

The judge turned to Paul's lawyer. "And you? Do you wish to say anything further?"

"No, Your Honor. I think it was all said yesterday. I have no witnesses to present."

"I declare a recess," the judge said. "I will retire to my chambers and come to a decision. Court will reconvene in one hour."

Richard turned to Andy. "I think we could use a cup of coffee and a Danish. Let's go to the cafeteria downstairs. They'll call us when we're needed."

They were in the cafeteria for just over an hour when they were called back into the courtroom.

"I'll make this brief," the judge said. "Bail is denied. The prisoner will be held over for trial."

Paul turned pale. "Can't we appeal?" he asked the lawyer.

Roy Wendell looked at Paul with disbelief. "On what grounds? More lies? I don't think so." He gathered his things together and picked up his briefcase. "I'm no longer the lawyer on this case," he told Paul. "You'll have to find someone else to defend you."

He rose from his chair and left.

Two officers led a pale, dejected Paul out of the courtroom and back to jail.

It was December fifteen, and Andy's divorce had just become final. She felt as though tons of weight had just dropped from her.

She was free and looking forward to getting back to California to help Midge with plans for her wedding.

CHAPTER XXXII

It was Christmas Day. All the arrangements had been made for Midge's wedding. In back of Andy's home, the hugh terrace that hung over the ocean had been beautifully decorated. Seats that would accommodate seventy guests had been set up on either side of the aisle, and a red runner bordered with lights on either side of the aisle, ran the full length of the terrace.

The sun was beginning to set, and the sky was glorious. Bright shades of red and coral stood out from the blue ether, and spread across the horizon. Andy had never seen a sunset quite like it. The wind had kicked up just enough to send the waves crashing into the shore. Seagulls and pelicans were flying overhead, chatting with each other, blending in perfect harmony with the orchestra seated over at the side of the terrace.

Maddie and Sonny arrived yesterday afternoon at the same time as John's parents. They spent an enjoyable evening in the family room getting acquainted and looking forward to the festivities of today.

As Andy looked around, she couldn't help thinking how well everything had worked out. Just one thing was missing. Andy dismissed it. It was too late for her and Jim.

Caterers were working in the kitchen preparing food for the reception that would be held by the swimming pool after the ceremony. Delicious aromas floated through the air and out to the patio. There was plenty of room on the spacious terrace for the dancing to be held during the reception.

Andy was all dressed, ready to take her place as Matron Of Honor.

Midge insisted that she wear a lovely, white silk suit that she picked out for her, and this puzzled Andy. She thought only the bride wore white. But when she protested, she could see that Midge was disappointed, so she gave in. After all, this was Midge's special day, and Andy was determined not to let anything spoil it for her.

She was on her way to the bedroom to help Midge dress when the doorbell rang.

"I'll answer that," one of the ushers offered.

Andy continued to the bedroom. Midge was just coming out of the shower. Her lovely, white wedding dress hung by the door, ready for her to put on.

"Has John arrived yet?" she asked Andy.

"I think I heard his voice. One of the ushers answered the doorbell."

Midge's hands shook as she pulled on her underwear and hose. "I'm nervous," she told Andy. "I don't know why. I've never been so sure of anything in my whole life as I am about John. I love him so much."

Andy smiled. "I know you do. So do I. I'll be getting the son I never had." She sounded wistful. "You've made the right choice, Midge. I'm glad you'll never have to go through what I did when I made the terrible mistake of marrying Paul. I'm sorry, honey, that you had to suffer for it. I'm not the only one he treated badly. But that's all in the past, thank God. Things have a way of working out, don't they?"

"They sure do," Midge declared. "You never know what's waiting in the wings."

Andy was silent for a moment. "You sound just like Jim," she told her. "Those were his very words when we were on the ship. I thought then that I wanted Paul to come back to me, but he said he thought Paul's leaving was the best thing that could have happened. You said the same thing when he left me. You were both right. Looking back on it, I think I was afraid to admit I had made a mistake. I did, you know - the biggest mistake of my life. It's too bad we don't get a chance to do it over again. I'd do it all so differently." She straightened her shoulders and smiled. "No sense brooding over it. What's done is done."

Was Midge smiling that special smile again? She looked so self-satisfied - as though she were hiding a secret. What is going on in that head of hers? Andy wondered.

Midge was dressed by now, and never looked more beautiful.

One of the ushers called through the door and informed them that the guests had all arrived and were seated on the terrace.

The wedding was about to begin.

Andy reached into her purse and handed something to Midge. "Here," she said. "You have something old, something new, something borrowed, and now you have something blue."

Midge opened the small box and looked at her mother in wide-eyed wonder. There, lying in the satin fold, was a pair of sapphire earrings surrounded by tiny diamonds. She had loved these since she was a child. "Oh, Mom!" she exclaimed.

"My mother gave these to me," Andy told her. "They'll look beautiful with your wedding gown, and I know you'll cherish them in the years to come."

"But, Mom, you've always loved these. Are you sure you want me to have them?"

"I wouldn't be giving them to you if I didn't. I've been saving them for you, and this is the perfect occasion. Wear them and enjoy them." She hugged her daughter. "I love you, Midge. Have a very happy life. I know you will with John."

As she opened the bedroom door she could hear the soft buzz of conversation above the orchestra. She took her place at the French doors that led to the terrace.

John was waiting with the minister. He looked so handsome in his tuxedo she felt a ripple of pride, knowing he would soon be her son-in-law.

One of the ushers offered her his arm, and Andy started her walk down the aisle. She had just taken her place in front of the minister when the band started playing the Wedding March.

Andy looked back as Midge appeared in the doorway. Then she saw something that caught her completely off guard!

Jim walked over to Midge and held out his hand to her. Midge looked up at him, an adoring look on her face, and took his arm. Andy had no idea he was here. But of course! Why wouldn't he be? He was Midge's father. Strange it had never occurred to her that Jim would be walking Midge down the aisle.

She had asked Midge about it once, but was told it had been taken care of. Since then she had been so involved with her divorce and Paul's trial that she hadn't thought to ask her about it again.

Why didn't Midge warn her? This was the first time Andy had seen Jim since he left the hospital in such a hurry after finding out that Midge was his daughter. Her knees threatened to buckle as she tried desperately to gain control. Her heart pounded so loud she thought it could be heard clear across the ocean to Catalina Island.

She looked at John for an explanation, but he was busy gazing at Midge as she walked down the aisle toward him. Andy felt as though she were dreaming.

But this was no dream.

This was real, and Jim was really here.

Jim and Midge finally reached the end of the aisle where the minister was waiting.

Jim took his place beside Andy. He looked down at her and smiled.

Andy's heart pounded even faster, if that was possible.

The band stopped playing and there was a moment of silence. Why didn't the minister start the ceremony? Startled, Andy looked at him, then back at Jim.

They were both smiling at her.

What is going on?

Then Jim took her hand in his and spoke. "Andy, I love you. I've always loved you. Will you do what you should have done years ago? Will you marry me?"

Andy's mouth fell open. She gulped. "N-now? H-here?" she stammered.

"Now," he replied. "Here. Will you Andy?"

She tried to answer but her voice was caught somewhere in her throat. Finally she was able to speak. "Oh, Jim! Yes!"

Jim put his arm around her and pulled her up beside Midge and John, who were beaming.

So was the minister. "Shall we begin?" he asked them.

"What about the license?" Andy asked.

"That's been taken care of," Jim assured her.

In a daze, Andy remembered the document Richard had asked her to sign just before they left for New York and the hearing. That must have been the license!

With stars in her eyes, she nodded to the minister, and the ceremony began.

It was all over in ten minutes, and Andy was now Mrs. James Rogers.

As the four of them walked back up the aisle together, Andy could swear that her feet never touched the floor.

She caught a glimpse of Richard, who had a broad grin on his face. He knew all along, and he never said a word!

Some reporters that Midge had invited congratulated Andy, and rushed to the phone to spread the news that Andy Jordan had just married her high school sweetheart - her daughter's real father.

After the wedding, dinner was served, the wedding cake was cut, and Midge and John, and Andy and Jim began the first dance. Soon the terrace was filled with guests joining the dancing.

In a few minutes Midge and John slipped into the bedroom to change their clothes. After many congratulations and goodbyes they left for their honeymoon aboard the same ship that Andy and Jim had sailed.

The guests lingered for a while, but gradually drifted away, and Andy and Jim were alone.

"I haven't planned much of a honeymoon," Jim said. "I wanted to ask you first where you'd like to go, but Midge didn't want me to spoil the surprise." He took her in his arms and kissed her. "Mrs. Rogers - where would you like to go for a honeymoon?"

"How about spending a few days at your home in Santa Barbara?" Andy suggested. "I've never seen it. It's a little late to drive there now. We could spend the night here, and leave in the morning. Then - well - do you have any ideas?"

Jim reached into his pocket and pulled out two tickets. "I picked these up two days ago. If this doesn't suit you, they can be changed."

Andy glanced at them, then at Jim. "Not on your life!" she exclaimed. "A cruise through Scandinavia! The one place where our cruise didn't go! How did you know I've always wanted to go there?" She tilted her head to one side and peered up at him. "Midge told you!"

"So it's okay with you?" he asked. "The ship sails from New York in two days. Do you think you can be ready?"

Andy laughed. "I'm ready now!" She examined the tickets and threw her arms around him. "Denmark - Sweden - Norway -- " she exclaimed. "Even Finland and Russia! Oh, Jim, I don't deserve this." She grinned. "But I'll take it! I love it!"

"I have something else for you," he said. He reached into his pocket and handed her a small, velvet box. "I couldn't give you this before. It would have spoiled the surprise."

Andy opened it. Inside was a beautiful engagement ring with a center diamond of three carats, surrounded by tiny diamonds that matched the wedding ring Jim slipped on her finger during the ceremony. "Oh, Jim! It's beautiful!"

"Let me put it on you," Jim said, gazing at her tenderly.

Suddenly he swept her up in his arms and carried her into the bedroom. "I've waited long enough for this," he told her as he placed her on the bed.

Soon they were cuddled under the covers. She had yearned to be in his arms for such a long time, and now she was.

He kissed her, gently at first, then with deep passion. They were both carried away with the deep ecstacy of a first love that had finally found its fulfillment. They were together again as they should have been all those years, and had recaptured the once-in-a-lifetime love they thought they had lost.